For Paul.
Creativity reigns.

To order additional copies of this book, contact:
Xlibris Corporation
1-888-795-4274
www.Xlibris.com
Orders@Xlibris.com

AGAVE NECTAR

Mexico has loaned me her poncho
Turned the water to tequila
I am Scorpion-stung and swollen
With her stories, her smells,
Her truth - intoxicating

Losing Fear
In every winding, one-way
Crumbling verdant street,
I see the souls of many through
My own eyes opened
The size of grapes in the market

    My love affair with this country began when I was young, perhaps just five years old. I preferred the sites, colours, the sounds, the ancientness of it, the heat, to my native country, Canada. Growing up in Vancouver, BC was a multicultural pedagogy. I knew about Mexico's coffee, tequila and chocolate before I came for the first time.

    For over one year, I lived in Guadalajara. I taught 5th Grade full-time, as well as evening classes in Yoga and Adults ESL at the Honda factory near Salto, about 1 hour out of the Centro. I lived in a traditional Mexican middle-class Colonia, or neighbourhood. I learned to speak the language from talking with my besinos (neighbours) I biked to school for 7:30 am each day and returned from the day's events between 6 pm and 9 pm most evenings. I worked just like a Mexican. I loved my sabbatical.

    I find there is as much acceptance of the fabulous, the mystical, the elaborate in Mexico, as there is the commonplace, the mundane. There is no fighting it, no judgments made. I weave three distinct themes together in 'Avenida', in a fabled vein, as if anything is possible.

    These are stories from the road, woven together, some in truth, and some in fiction.

-**Rachel**

'Brother blood, brother blood
We're of the same spirit, of the same mud
Brother blood, brother blood
We're from the same water, we're from the same love

I've got scars from livin', scars from love
Strike me dead if I'm lyin'
I've got brothers below, and brothers above
With all of our blood we are tryin'
I keep tryin' for everything
It comes a piece at a time
I've got a mountain I'm determined to climb

But I took the heat, created a beat
And I've got the heart of a lion
I've got friends who are dead, friends in jail
I've got friends who are policemen
And the girls I know now, the girls I knew then
I still make my music to please them
I keep tryin' for everything
I don't count the cost
But I see an ocean I'm determined to cross
'Cause I took the heat, created the beat
And I've got the strength of a dragon

I've got drums of the jungle, drums of the street
Drums of the Indian chief
I've got the fire of the gospel, a river of blues
And I got the soul of belief
And I keep tryin' for everything
It's been a long, long road
I've got a song that's about to explode
I was born to the beat that pounds like the heat
And I've got the drums of the spirit.'

The Neville Brothers - 'Brother Blood'

by: Leah Robinson

AVENIDA DE LOS MAESTROS
Based on a true story.

Cover art by

Haley Marshall

Chapter 1

Profundo

'The scrupulous and the just, the noble,

humane, and devoted natures;

the unselfish and the intelligent

may begin a movement

-but it passes away from them.

They are not the leaders of a revolution. They are its victims.'

-Joseph Conrad,

'Under Western Eyes' circa 1911, (ch.3)

Elisa shook her oft-foiled golden tonsorial splendor one last time that sunny Guadalajara morning and headed out to her SUV ML 500 Mercedes, also gold. She strutted, a tigress, even when she swept the front of their Providencia home. Always heels, often gold snakeskin, her favourites in a massive collection. She did this, while her maid, Sofia, worked her 74-year-old nails to the bone inside Elisa's castle. Elisa only ever swept the front. She did this to ensure the neighbours would see that she was both proprietor and grounds keeper. Every detail of her life to the 'T', an Agenda of Folly, it needed to be like that for Senora Elisa Osegura Vazquez.

That day, she was to meet three of her allies, the only three who understood Elisa's need to be five steps ahead of the game. It was Hairstyling Day, Thursday. She had six hours until Juan returned from the day's events. She would prepare a *pollo con mole rojo* (classic Mexican chicken breasts, baked in a red chili/chocolate sauce) for him, later make love with him, allowing him manly free reign, in the hopes this coming Saturday might be Diamond Bracelet Day.

She entered Frida's, her hair stylist's, in a haughty cape of respirated grandeur. There it was: her makeshift homeland. Her Breathing Room. This day was mother's milk in the life of Elisa. She scanned Nayeli, Noemi and Lupita. *Las Diosas*. (The Godesses) *Las Tenidas de Secretos*. (The Keepers of Secrets)

A rain of enthused kisses and sisterly exchanges of 'Buenos dias, Mija!' followed. Elisa felt herself take a deep breath and pseudo-relax into Frida's familiar chair. She would be first, as the others sipped their espressos. She was always first; it was implied. Nayeli moved away from the others to chat with her, but Elisa felt herself slipping. She had been up for too many hours, been worried for too many days. God, Elisa needed rest. She couldn't fight it, falling into a dreamy oblivion, into Frida's *preciosa* finger tips. This was Zapopan, in the treed, traffic-calmed, Hummer haven of North-West Guadalajara.

There was free license to be loosened of her life's many secret *picardias* (dirty tricks) for just a moment. Sanctuary. She was Culpable. Yet she would be Beautiful at all times, come Hell or high water. Elisa's infinite vial of beauty made her life make some kind of sense, physically validating the superficial edifice she and Juan had erected as their daily camouflage.

She heard Noemi going into a recitative about how good a little auburn would be in Elisa's mane. Then, onto a schoolyard issue that had arisen between their two sons, Chava and Octavio. Elisa tried so hard to stay awake enough to respond to Noemi's imperatives (also implied).

It was to no avail. Octavio was feeling the obvious strain of the position of his 9-year-old life and had been throwing dirt at Chava resultantly. Her mind began to move to random places, she felt herself dozing: 'Did I asked Sofia to take extra special care to water each plant and shine the leaves of the banana tree with a chamois?' Elisa was circling the drain. 'Grapes. I like grapes. Should Octavio get a puppy?' She would sleep through her streaks.

Noemi continued on. If she had no audience with Elisa, the others would surely want to know about the boys' antics.

Elisa awoke some time later to her head being gently caressed into Hair Drying Blow-Out Position 1. Three other Providencia women had entered the salon and were having a serious discussion about properties for sale outside Manzanillo, it being The *Best* Time to Buy. Bleary-eyed and still somewhat dozy, it was hard to make out what they were saying. Elisa began to come back into being slowly. 'Sticky mouth', she thought. 'Need another coffee. And a lime water.'

It was implied, as Frida returned with both, aligning Elisa's sleepy, freshly-tinted head for Product Finishing.

Elisa knew as clear as day she could have any man she wanted. She was a true stunner: powerful, gorgeous, smart. Juan was her pick. He called her 'Serpente' because she undulated gracefully as she moved. Elisa could slither out of any situation. Anyone near her had best wield a large stick for protection, as Elisa was prone to hissing and taking venomous bites at random turns.

She came back to life in Frida's stylist chair once her head was elevated back to its usually-alert position. Elisa was a bright woman, and like so many, she was drawn to drama, like a moth to a flame. She had to balance this irrational part of her life with a heightened sense of awareness at all times, it was par for the course. As she felt herself revitalizing somewhat from the hair service, her ears pricked up. She could hear a gaggle of women gossiping loudly and discussing Manzanillo real estate. For a moment, Elisa was struck by the emphatic sentiments spilled forth from each, in a circulating manner, loud tones. Elisa had come to unwind, just for a precious moment. These Others were wrecking it for her. She became annoyed. The serpent was rising.

'They are causing Mexican soil to be pock-marked with blood. The *rios* (rivers) are contaminated with death and violence! Our children are not safe!'

'*They* get all the best reservations in town while *we* have to wait in line. And what do other nations think of this proud land now? What kind of reputation does this Narco Traficante impress upon the rest of the world? That we are merely purveyors of white powder? '

'We have to live in fear. Surely these crooks will overthrow the *policia Mexicano*! Yes, Nayeli! What about the true spirit of our Mexico?'

'Indeed, Pancho Villa would surely roll is his grave! We have lost our heritage to this villain!'

And there it was: an instant of exhaustion, fear, frustration and blind rage catapulted Elisa. She went from her neo-meditative dream world to Serpente as fast as a line could be snorted. Up she shot, out of Frida's caring manos.

In three strong strides across the floor, Elisa made her target. She pulled the revolver out of her purse and aimed it at the stylist who was getting ready to colour the Pancho Villa's fan's mane.

'Shave her head. Shave her head <u>right now</u> or I will shoot you!' she bellowed. No one moved. A silence seeped through the salon like a serpentine fog curling through the early morning streets of Guadalajara after the rains.

'SHAVE HER HEAD, PUNTA MADRE! You heard me!' Elisa barked in her Spanish, rolling the r on the last part of 'madre' for dramatic effect. The younger stylist, in fact Frida's niece, Juanita, shifted her feet slightly thinking this might somehow change the state of the nation.

Juanita remained frozen.

Elisa had the revolver cocked in her right hand, with her elbow bent, arm unrelenting. Without moving her arm, she pivoted her body. An expert master, the symphony conductor, she then aimed the shooter at the woman responsible for alluding to Pancho as separate from today's Mexican mega-industry of drug trafficking. In fact, Mexican history and a major lack of resources had brought on the desperate state.

She looked at the woman, her eyes narrowed. She swung one hip in a dominating stance of brazen power.

'You have no idea what you are talking about. You have no idea what Narco Traficante live. You have no concept of what it is to love a man through it all. No fucking idea.'

And to the young Juanita, Elisa steadied herself, 'You will shave her fucking head right now, or yours, too, will be blown off.' Elisa said this as if she were placing an order at Ochenta y Ocho, one of Guadalajara's finest eateries: calm, focused, serious; an appetite for more.

And so Juanita complied. Tress by tress the mermaid's muse, long, thick ebony locks fell to the floor as the gun held, as the hip upturned, as the gaze fixed.

* * * * * * * *

Juanita tried to stay on task. Her hand shook once at the very end of the shave when she contemplated who would care for her children if she died here. Juanita ruptured a snippet of skin accidentally as she lost her way in the thought.

The woman looked at her face in the mirror, no longer as radiant without her crowning glory. The woman could see her own indignant horror as it creased her forehead. As if in slow motion, the woman looked down, a sickening torrid shame creeping into her proud Mexican soul. A tiny drop of blood fell to the floor, next to the pile of hair.

Elisa turned on her heel.

As she pushed the door open with her left elbow, she turned to her audience. 'Keep your mouths shut or you will find yourself cursing the *rajas con crema* (dark green milder chili's cooked with caramelized white onions and cream) burning on your earthly stove from Heaven above!'

She didn't bother to pay for the service.

* * * * * * *

Chapter 2

Centro

'I wake to sleep, and take my walking slow.

I feel my fate in what I cannot fear.

I learn by going where I have to go.'

–Theodore Roethke circa 1908, from

'The Waking'

      In Centro, near a major tianguis, not far from the original trading site of the Aztecs which is called San Juan de Dios, up an obscure flight of stairs, in a tiny crumbling room with half a roof, rife with the odour of ancient urine, there lived a small boy whose name was Gustavo.

Gustavo lived alone, and had done since he could remember. He was told by the other children of the street many different things about his family. Some said he came from a family of kings, with riches galore, money falling out of their pockets, and that they had died in a plane crash off the coast of Mazatlan, their bodies never to be found again. Some said he was left there to make sure the cockroaches didn't eat the city whole. Some children told Gustavo that his mother would be back for him. The truth was Gustavo had no family any longer. He fended for himself, foraging the streets for food. The other street urchins told him these stories to give him Hope. Gustavo was a part of Centro, in the Hidalgo region, Guadalajara's downtown area, a tiny, 7-year-old, as consequential to the country as a mite picked out of his colchon. He was, like so many other children who were left the same way, smiling through and trying to make good on life.

Gustavo wasn't sure if his mother named him 'likable one', or if his adopted street sister, Ana Lisa had given him that name. Ana Lisa was 14. She didn't have money or time to cook for Gustavo and neither of them had a stove, but she looked over him as best she could. Ana Lisa had been left the same way. She had realized that her mother was not coming back for her-ever. Once her breasts matured at 13, she began her young life as a prostitute on the streets on Centro. Her cheap sex could be bought as easily as the Halloween masks, the shoes, the mariachi costumes, the hand-woven baskets on Juarez Ave. And so it was. Ana Lisa had a subsistence income through a life of crime she never chose.

Ana Lisa had decided Gustavo should be named this as she felt his soul was full of a pure kind of love she could no longer conjure. Her soul had hardened and become numb in the act of survival, but she remembered it being more open once. She loved little Gustavo for being beautiful, smart, kind and bold, a piece of art she could tend for free, one lovely thing to behold in a dire landscape.

So they were friends for life, each looking out for the other. Ana Lisa had a mattress, but no place for it. She stashed the mattress under the stairs at the bottom of the entry to San Juan de Dios and hoped for the best each day. Once she had discovered a drunken homeless man sleeping on her mattress and had to ask him to leave. He had risen, a broken bottle in his hand and slammed it down on her head. She had been given a head injury which caused her to take information in more slowly after this happened. It was as if she expected something of this nature to happen someday, so she was less than surprised when her fate alighted.

She was grateful to have her mattress back, her only piece of real estate, stained with her own fresh blood. The scar had taken forever to heal, and she was left with a place on her head where her hair didn't grow fully. Ana Lisa was painfully embarrassed about the scar, a jagged streak of lightening on her head.

After that, she relied on Gustavo to make sure she was getting things straight. Neither child could read, but Gustavo was known to be smart. She double-checked most things with him, like when Sunday mass would get out so that she could hold her hand out to the grateful masses, or confirmed rumours of the Night Raids where the policia would come to gentrify Centro by scooping busloads of strays and taking them off into the hills, far from the main city. She never knew what time it was, but Gustavo could tell by making a sundial of his small hands at one specific point, outside Teatro Delgado.

Every time she needed to know, she would think extra hard about her friend Gustavo, and he would simply come to her. It was a milagro they laughed about, but it seemed to happen every time. He felt it was her 'calling' to him, and he knew she needed to share with him. In a herd, one will compensate for another if weakness exists.

Ana Lisa could not risk being late for the mostly foreign men who plied her services for a mere handful of pesos. They asked for 'La Perla del Occidente', which was a double entendre, a backhanded compliment of the most lecherous kind. She was seen in their morose minds as a pearl, and the city itself is also called just that in tourist books.

They were doing their sundial clock trick at the tourist office near the east side of the theatre. It read 4:05 pm. Perfect. Ana Lisa would have time to unwrinkle her dress for her evening's events and perhaps try for a hustled taquito along the way. She would have given her right arm for a taquito at this point, dripping with carne asada, fresh cebola, fresh lime and cilantro. The head injury kept Ana Lisa thinking about the very minute she was in, keeping her wits about her. Planning wasn't always easy, as she ran into a block in her mind when she went beyond what was to transpire in the next 2 minutes.

'What happens tonight, Ana Lisa? Que onda? Will you come play Loteria with me before the sun disappears?' asked Gustavo, looking up hopefully at her pensive face.

'No, Gustavo. No games tonight. I must meet this next man at the steps of the Expiatoro at 5:30 pm. We can play tomorrow, but tonight I must work.'

Gustavo was disappointed, but fleeted away from the emotion quickly. They each did that. There had been so much disappointment in their young lives, such hurt in dealing with each day, they learned to get over it fast.

'Entonces, Ana Lisa, let me come to the mattress with a bucket of water and I can try to brush out your hair with my fingers.' She laughed, her head tilted right back as tinkly music of the spheres rang from her mouth, her jaw wide open revealing straight white teeth, sunbeams of the sunny tarde kissing her chocolate cheeks.

They walked through crowds of tourists, people doing errands, families of nine eating their Sunday afternoon ice cream cones. She joked with him as he skipped to keep up with her longer young woman strides. Team Ragamuffin.

They got to her mattress only to find a teenager in nice clothes peeing on it. Once the boy was done, he zipped up his pants and turned, eyes darting to see if anyone else had noticed. Ana Lisa and Gustavo could say nothing. Nothing on the street was truly theirs. They owned nothing. They simply stopped and stared.

'Vafangula!' the teenager hollered. 'You kids got nothing better to do than watch someone taking a pee?' Ana Lisa and Gustavo did not move. The boy wanted to get back to his Sunday group and had a squeaky clean girl to impress. He shoved past the two, ignorant of the territory he'd marked.

Ana Lisa sighed. The old mattress smell would be replaced by urine just as the smell of pozole had replaced the stench of the blood from her head over months of exposure near the stand. She straightened her outfit, a raggy mix of jumbled clothes she had found on the street. Her dress fit, but was becoming snug around her middle and breasts; her sweater said 'Hollister' on it and was far too big for her undernourished frame. Ana Lisa had claimed that after watching two young lovers kissing so passionately in the square, the boy had unzipped his hoody and let it fall from his shoulders. She had crept over and pulled it away quickly. The boy had been so taken up in the arms of his beloved, he hadn't noticed and the young couple had eventually moved through the noche to continue their fondling elsewhere. Ana Lisa had no shoes at all. She had not owned a pair in all of her 13 years.

The one item of value that Ana Lisa had, the one she would not lose was her Bolsa. Ana Lisa's Bolsa contained myriad shades of bright shiny eye colours in tiny pots that she had stolen from the cranky Mendoza couple at the tianguis, and for application purposes, a broken shard of mirror that had fallen off a left car mirror after one of the many crashes she'd witnessed in Centro. Also inside the Bolsa was a hot pink Max Factor lipstick that had been dropped absently by an older tourist lady as she had exited Ballet Folklorico last year.

Gustavo had spotted the miss and dove for the bounty, running back to Ana Lisa with the prize. She had taken a look at the colour, 'Perfecto, Gustavo! Este colore es perfecto para mi! Gracias, amigo!'

In truth, Ana Lisa was a genuine Mexican beauty with no need for the tart shade. She had designs on being a distant part of a lineage of hard-working, proud Mayans, her imagined descendants, though no one could tell her what her origins really were. But the hot pink she smeared on her young mouth, and the dramatic eyes she created for her nightly work allowed her to escape herself more easily; she saw the colours as her Night Costume. She wore them every time she was called 'La Perla'. She left the colour off her face when she wasn't turning tricks.

The two clambered out of the hole that was Ana Lisa's resting place under the stairs to avoid the fresh teen urine smell. They sat down on the third step and continued chatting as if there had been no intermission. Their lives were seemingly a series of hit and misses. They were learning a bizarre form of Zen tolerance living on these vibrant, musical streets.

'Ana Lisa, my belly is growing so hungry, I could vomit air, 'said Gustavo. We must find some food. I can go and be back soon.'

'OK, Pepino, but come say goodbye before 5:15 pm because it will take me some time to walk from here to the Expiatoro.'

'I will. I will try to find enough for each of us.'

And he was off, leaving Ana Lisa to perfect eye make-up application with her fingertip dipped in saliva. Gustavo moved like a river, easily dodging the crowd. He did, in fact, envision his lithe body as *Rio de Los Calles*, the River of the Streets. He could sense danger and tried to stay back from it, taking only what he needed. He was not greedy about it most times, but he felt his brain slipping as the hunger grew.

Gustavo found a spot, up on a bench, slightly above the crowd. Affecting his most endearing self, he cooed, '5 pesos para mi lonche, por fav! Soy niño sin dinero.' ('5 pesos for my lunch, please! I'm a boy without money.') It seemed in the hustle most looked past him, or looked but simply moved on. Gustavo waited and hoped, waited and hoped.

He began to shake with hunger and the time was moving on and on. Gustavo prayed for a small *milagro* (miracle) to come to him. Every second ticked by as if in slow motion, the heat was unrelenting in the late afternoon sunshine of Centro. He noted a stunning woman, stepping out of a double-parked gold SUV ML 500 Mercedes. In his state of raw hungry vulnerability, she appeared as if in a movie, her stature etched into his burning corneas by the halcyon back light. How he wished his own mother was that woman, there to collect him and take him away from this. He ran towards her, staggering absently a little, not sure what he wanted at this point, only moving with the instinct of hunger.

The woman moved as if she had business to take care of. Striding towards a stall of flowers on the street, it was clear she was not there to linger. But Gustavo felt himself drawn to her. He used his last energy of the day to stumble over to where she was.

He managed to get close enough to look into Elisa's eyes. She was captivating, an oasis in the crowd. He tugged at the end of her long evening shawl, 'Please, Hermosa! Por fa-'

But the child was cut off brusquely. 'Stay away from me. I have nothing for you.' Elisa barked, used to those who clambered to get her riches. She pulled her shawl back in a swift motion and kept moving.

As he turned to solicit a new passerby, a wild old woman with a wandering eye and a deep scar just below it lunged towards him with her cane waving in the air, fire in her eyes. 'Cuidate en este parte del ciudad, niño! Los lobos son aquí con nosotros. Es verdad. Cuidate. Eres valiente' ('Be careful in this part of the city, small boy. The wolves are here with us. It's true. Take care. Be valiant.') And she was off, like a shaggy night beast.

Gustavo wasn't entirely certain whether he had just imagined these characters, if his mind was beginning to play famished tricks on him. He was delusional with the hunger, parasites munching his insides. As he imagined her speeches to other random strangers, he began to feel very woozy, almost delirious with famine. The heat of the endless day caused streams of sweat down his back, his clothing sticking to him. He was desperate by this time. He would miss Ana Lisa if he didn't get some nourishment and return to her soon.

Gustavo jumped down, almost tumbling in the process, so dizzy was the tiny man from too many days of going without. He was being watched. From across the courtyard, his every vulnerability was being absorbed by Bettos, the head corral leader. Bettos would wait until just the right moment, as the boy could not wait any longer to swoop in vulture-like.

Gustavo ran to Mama Rosa at her taquito stand.

'Please can I….please can you help me? I am only a small boy, with no home, no money. I need food.'

Mama Rosa looked kindly on the child, but there was no way. If she gave to this one child, how could she not give to the swarms of others? This would surely drown her frail business.

'No, Precioso, I cannot. I do not have the resources to give to you.' she replied, pushing a steaming fresh handful of goodness to her next customer.

Gustavo felt the swelling wave of frustration, bewilderment and heat exhaustion rising in him might take him completely.   He could not do this for another moment. Gustavo felt himself, his entire being going flaccid as a washed up jellyfish. He was spinning, spinning, down…he felt himself falling through the crowd to the ground.

And just as he almost landed, a slim strong hand was there to steady him. It was the most reassurance the boy had ever felt. He was still dizzy, but now he felt his breath return. Bettos felt the reptilian draw of power rush to the front of his brain, as he did with every conquest. Now was his time.

'You need some food,' the man spoke gently to Gustavo. 'Here, let me buy you a few taquitos and an *agua fresca* (fruit juice flavoured water). Do you like coconut or lemon agua fresca?'

The thought of nourishment of any kind at that dire moment simply *sent* Gustavo. He could hardly put words together, so parched was he from this business of running to save himself. He imagined a lemon agua fresca going down his throat, how good that would be.

'Mmm…m. Lemon.' He mumbled, scarcely able to form the words in his dry *boca* (mouth).

Within moments, the icy-sweet beverage was handed to him, the very scent of it a relief. He took a sip, life returning to his lithe body. A few minutes later, Bettos returned with two taquitos, their oily scent holding a place in Heaven for Gustavo. He wolfed them down, feeling his blood sugar take a rapid flight back to a normal state. The world around him settled again.

Bettos chuckled, 'Better, huh? Lemon is my favourite also.'

Gustavo just stared at the man. Why had this man come to help him? What time was it now? Where was Ana Lisa?

'Do you know what time it is?' Gustavo asked.

'5:10 pm,' Bettos replied, looking at his watch. 'Why should time matter at all to a small niño like you?'

'I am supposed to meet my friend to walk with her.'

'Let your body rest, young man. You need a minute. What is your name?'

'Gustavo,' he replied, looking at the stranger, feeling good physically but still unsettled.

Bettos had an eerie cut that had formed a mass of scar tissue on his upper left lip that fixated Gustavo. The man's eyes moved a lot, it seemed he had a busy brain, Gustavo thought.

'What's yours?'

'I am Bettos. It is a pleasure to know you, pequeño Gustavo.'

Gustavo just looked at Bettos, immobilized for a minute. He knew there was something strange about this situation. He wasn't sure how to manage it, never having encountered such kindness before.   'I have to go. I must meet Ana Lisa. Thank you for your kindness, Señor.'

Off he ran, his skinny legs with their knocked knees splaying side to side as he scurried off. Bettos watched him intently. He would find the child again soon, the perfect candidate for such a difficult job.

* * * * * * *

Chapter 3

Comidas

'I want God, I want poetry,

I want danger, I want freedom,

I want goodness, I want sin.'

-Aldous Huxley, 1914

––––––––

'That which thy fathers have bequeathed to thee, earn it anew if thou wouldst possess it.'

-Goethe: from 'Faust'

Elisa arrived back at her home in Providencia, her Colonia, nestled in the breezy trees of the Northern upscale end of Guadalajara at 6:10 pm that Tuesday evening. She had shaken off the events of earlier that day at the salon, with just enough time to finish putting the details on the evening's meal, so called the ceña. It was essential that she kept resilient; not only to keep her coiffure in place but also to ensure that their life secrets were kept in their tomes. She loved to cook. It was one of the only grounding activities in her life, allowing her to remain unshaken, or apparently so.

Elisa was devoted to her boy, Octavio and to her husband of 12 years, her sweetheart, Juan. The only two domestic activities in her home that she saved for herself were cooking for her boys and the sweeping of the front area. Everything else was taken care of by her 73-year-old maid, Sofia. Elisa had figured out just how each item in the front area should be placed in order to facilitate the stream of money, health and happiness that entered the home.

Elisa was determined that money, health and happiness would be a constant in her familial life.

Elisa also used The Front Sweep as her meditative moment each day. It served her in another way: it allowed her to survey the minutia and the comings and goings on her street, creating an equally fine show of her latest purchase of fancy Plaza de Gallerias sandals for passing onlookers. In the event of a disturbance or delivery related to Juan's business, she remained ahead of most of it, utilizing the front sweep foil to full advantage. As well, it gave Hernando, the elderly retired neighbour to their left a clear view of her flawless Pilates-perfected backside. Thus, everyone was happy.

She used her time in the cocina differently. The time she took to prepare their dinner was a time of deeper thought, a letting down of her guard; a quiet haven for Elisa. She had learned a great deal about food, its importance and how to cultivate raw ingredients into delicacy. She had cultivated herself and the Who she had become with the same degree of care. Her family would eat well every night. This was less about being a good Mexican wife to Juan and mother to Octavio in the traditional sense, and more about the celebration of abundance that was hers in the end.

* * * * * * * *

She had grown up the eleventh daughter of a taxi driver in a dusty, outlying portion of Zapopan in Guadalajara in the 1980s. Her father was a good driver, but he had not stayed faithful to her mother, taking up with one of his clients one day, never to return to them. By the time Elisa was 14, she had left home. It made more sense to her than living on crumbs her mother salvaged from the backs of restaurants to feed 11 children. Her mother never searched for Elisa, no police report was filed. The child had flown the nest. This was accepted. This must be accepted by many women in Mexico, by both the birds that fly and the mothering hens. This is the way it goes commonly.

Elisa had run to the Ex-convento del Carmen, which had been the central nuns convent in the downtown core of Guadalajara. It had been converted, just as the previous decades of nuns had cemented Catholic religious conversion amidst its ancient walls. The Ex-convento now served as an artistic Mecca. It had been converted to a movie theatre, screening subtitled pictures of merit, mostly film noir.

At the time of Elisa's fugitive state, it had still been a 'convent' in the true sense of the word and the nuns had taken young Elisa in without question. She was kept safe in the convent with the Sisters, given a daily role in the kitchen, chopping and sweeping each day as her requisite gracias del Dios. She lived there comfortably for a period of four months before deciding it was ultimately too limiting for her.

After that, Elisa had moved on to work in the front of the house at a popular eatery, using her God-given assets to turn the heads of her patrons at Estacion de Lulio in the up market Chapultepec region of the city. And gorgeous she was. She was noted for her beauty by men and women, even children stopped their crying in the streets when they looked on Elisa.

The owner, Domingo, could see she would be the perfect garnish for his dishes. The food was already renowned and so it became a most fortunate move on his part: she was a hard worker with a willingness of task unusual for a girl her age. Elisa kept her focus on her regular clientele and smiled under even the most extreme circumstances in the restaurant. Soon she moved on to be head server. By the time Elisa was 16, she was virtually managing one of the more successful loncherias in Guadalajara. Elisa had her own tiny, dingy rental apartment, just across the street from the restaurant. She could be seen skipping off to work most days, the first to be there in the morning mist, the last to leave as the palms swayed down Libertad and the men wiped the sweat of toil from their brows, leaving Centro construction sites, pelicaria's and taco stands.

It would not have been Lulio without her.

Estacion de Lulio had a history of its own. The café had been a library years before and the owner had decided to keep some of its original charm. The walls and ceiling remained as they had been through history, aged to classical comfort. It had taken the name 'Lulio' after the writer, alchemist, mystic theologist, Raimundo Lulio (1235 – 1315). Domingo was an open-minded man, a free-thinker himself, with a gregarious demeanor and a gentlemanly way. He took most of his liberal cues from his wife, Esme, a heavy smoker of both Las Botas Mexican cigarettes and 'la mota' (marijuana).

Esme loved to talk with the patrons. Domingo and Esme both embraced the philosophy espoused by Lulio in their partnership, *'the common man thinks only a little, with almost no profound depth-almost no analytical system of thought'*. This ideology was palpable in each dish. Scrumptious food and just as likely was a meeting of uncommon minds at the front bar. Some said it embodied progress in Mexico. Books were written, ideas sparked, romances culminated or terminated. Lulio was where it was at.

While Lulio himself was a native of Palma de Mallorca in fact, off the coast of Spain, the couple had decided years back they would some day bring his liberating ideas to their own native city, Guadalajara. It stood, popular with modern artists, philosophers, bi-sexuals and radicals of the new Mexico. It attracted many wealthy business owners and politicians, real estate developers and lawyers as well. The bohemian feeling in the establishment made everyone welcome. Left and right met under the common umbrella of food and music.

Elisa had seen she would need to make a New Day for her own life when she fled her insubstantial family of origin. Lulio had been a haven for her, a place she could rebel in classic adolescent style, while blossoming as a creature of lasting ebullient succulence. She was supported there, adored. It filled the need for 'family' that had been lost when she had been abandoned by her own parents. Her saltine tears dissipated as she grew into abundance.

Elisa harked back to those formative kitchen days in her mind in her modern home with Juan and Octavio. She attended to each mouth-watering detail, the *comidas* (food) ever-more important as she could not forget the lack of food in her younger years. Elisa took a moment away from her enchilada assembly for that evening to arrange the fresh-cut flowers she had scuttled down to the 24-hour flower market, outside the graveyard, off Avenida de Los Maestros and *calle* (street) Enrique Diaz de Leon to purchase for her men's glorious dinner table.

This was a matter of pride. She knew that in North America her domestic role might have been laughable. She might have been interpreted as a Luddite or an unevolved slave to her family, suffering from arrested development. She didn't see it that way. It was about honouring what her life held now.

The flower market in Guadalajara itself saw more action than the emergency ward at the hospital. It was there so that anyone anytime, anywhere in the average 12 -14 hour Mexican work day could take a moment to buy flowers to lay on the graves of their dead. It was there for wedding-planning, for friendships that deserved celebrating. It was always busy; open through the night for new babies, for sweethearts. There to remind the citizens what their own lives were for. There to celebrate the unions that humans have allowing daily lives to be enriched by another soul. The flower market was busiest around Dia de los Muertes (Day of the Dead), when it is common practice for Mexican family and friends to buy flowers for the deceased and lay them on graves, often sleeping through the night on this auspicious occasion to commemorate those whose souls are with us, but who have left earth in physical form.

Sofia, Elisa's maid, could often be seen there and then walking slowly towards the nearby graveyard, her head down. She was missing many: children, a husband, sisters, parents, lovers. She would sit into the night missing.

Elisa arranged massive pink Cala lilies, alongside tuberoses and ginger flower buds, humming along to the Julieta Venegas song she heard coming from the radio. 'Limon y Sal', a common favourite in all her country rang in her ears. She chirped along with it, happy to be in the sanctuary of her villa, far away from the madding crowds in the dusty streets of the bustling city. Juan kept his little butterfly in a cocoon of safety and quietude there. He knew what she needed; part of Juan's work on the planet was To Know. He was about digging to the depth. He knew what his princess thrived on. He tried to give her what she'd not known before.

She had morphed into her present life some time ago, and, as in the heart of any woman abandoned by family, a part was stuck. It would be forever difficult to bypass the scars of her youth. Almost Neitzsche-esque, Elisa appeared grand in the halcyon shadow cast by the afternoon sun: 'That which does not kill me makes me stronger.'

Transcendence is the river whose current draws the damaged soul. We are given as many pains as we are creative gifts.

'...no me gusta tu forma de ver', ('I don't like the way you look') Julieta's voice soft as fresh-ground lemony cinnamon floated through their mansion. She had sound everywhere in her kitchen with the eight speakers Juan had strategically assembled to ensure Elisa's listening pleasure while domesticating. Juan knew, too, Elisa's maternal and very female needs. He adored his wife, lavishing her with praise each night, putting his best efforts into securing her every day comforts. He knew she missed her family of origin, he knew she sucked back on her tears for her family now, in order to keep going. He loved her for being brave despite it all. He loved her dignity. Elisa had not deserved what had transpired in her family before.

Juan himself had seen some hardship, emerging from a life of street rodentry to becoming a Prince in the cartel world. While his vocation was smattered in ugly blackness, he remained top in the chain, an expert in trafficking, in dealing with the multitude of earthly horrors that came along with it.

Both souls united in the promise of a better day. It was not like any Mexican had a lot of choice. It's still the same story. Upward mobility in the semi-developing world nation was as tough as swimming in molasses. Corruption from every angle ensured thwarted movement; most found this to be so disheartening they gave up. If it's enabled to continue, corruption will cause arrested development in any situation, from the growth of a country to the flourishing of a marriage. The rare soul stayed the course to graduate a doctor or a lawyer in Guadalajara. It was considered one of the best-educated regions of the country. Even then, job security and work itself was stymied by corruption within the so-called 'systems'. Organization at the most basic of levels didn't have a history of being a strong point amidst the spontaneous life of Mexico.

Yes, their life was very tricky.

But it had its just desserts.

Some days, Elisa felt she could not be paid enough to manage what she, the supporting wife had to deal with. Elisa was grateful for her refuge, as every day held enough anxiety inside the woman to power a small plane to San Francisco.

'Yo te quiero con Lim-on y Sal...' ('I want you with Lem-on and Salt') the melody went on, greeted by the trumpet of the bridge in the tune. Elisa knew the words only to well. While she had attained wealth and status as a Mexican woman of privilege as a result of her choices and her incomparable visage, Elisa was, like most in her native land disappointed. In the things she'd missed. In the way her homeland caused her to skirt honesty and cultivate façade in order to survive. In a place where corruption reveals yet more insidious layers of corruption, many choices she knew were afforded women in the developed world were just not hers to play with.

Elisa made good on the cards fate dealt her. She played rough, in the face of rough play. Juan felt her energy in his heart upon the very thought of her and could only try his best to ensure she did not bleed or suffer on account of him.

He tried to secure her, to adore her, to enrapture his beloved. While he had also been born into squalor, he had vowed not to follow that route. If he had no choice, he would *invent* choice. This was his musing as a young man: he saw that Mexico's blood had been shed, battle after battle, the women of the country lost in rape and war to so many other invading countries. He saw the scraps the US had left Mexico and felt the gurgle of hatred ride in him, irrational but a virtual part of the DNA of any nationalist who had seen generations pillaged by outsiders. Juan looked on his dangerous life choices as a product of desperation, punctuated with a sprinkle of vengeance towards the invaders that had destroyed Mexico's chances, over and over again. Just as Mexico got her Independence, attempting to stand on shaky legs, she was invaded-again.

This lingering ire was present in many modern-day Mexicans, most tangible in the corridor that ran from Puerto Vallarta to Guadalajara. This area was rife with trafficking, in part the enmity housing a heartburning number of educated people as well. Here, intellect and drugs pushed Mexico upward, side by side, partly in battle with one another, partly in unison. For what other means could push the fraught nation forward?

Still, intelligent, perceptive Elisa noted tiny details surrounding their life and thus endured larger storms than her husband could have ever imagined. Part of the strange brew that was her life was her sensitivity. She put on a brave face, but she thirsted for peace every day. She had to accept the state of the nation: the life she had was not without sacrifice.

Perhaps it was the essence of machismo that coated Juan's being that centered her, balanced her delicate heart. She was a product of her environment. Elisa had fallen for Juan as we all do: irrationally, inextricably. She had been overtaken by desire for her man, as if this was what she would need as a match for her own yin: his protective virility, his yang. They lived out the machismo sexism that is commented on by many a traveler to Mexico. Certainly, this was typical.

She was as Woman as a Georgia O'Keefe, the intoxicating juxtaposition of the calyx of the fresh-cut flower next to the street smog it's sold on.

The other piece, the underbelly, was the sheer facts and the breakneck pace of each day for a Narco-married woman in a land of tumult. A boatload of musings greeted dear Elisa each morning as she sipped her torrificada sugar-roasted dark coffee, her mind percolating wonder about her life, her man and her child.

No day in the existence of Elisa Mariana Osegura Vazquez was without a good and proper mindfuck.

Still, as we all do in the end, she strengthened what remained. Elisa plied whatever she could via her Place in the world. Finally, she had a Place for herself, no longer one of many mouths to feed. Her Place was with her powerful Juan (her only boy, Octavio, a testament to her rebellion). She would not repeat a life of no restraint on childbearing the way her naïve mother had, the way so many Mexican women are encouraged to breed by the church, by their husbands, by survivalist lovers taken on the side, by the very essence of *machismo*. She named her son 'eight' as the numeral itself expressed infinity when it was written horizontally. She had broken the spell of not having enough. Forever.

Elisa returned to her fresh chicken enchiladas, with avocado and cashews, the exotic nut of India also sold in Mexico. She worked to perfect the nutty creamy sauce as a gentle breeze of the *tarde* snaked under her nostrils. The light was getting lower, the sunset would descend as Juan arrived back home. Cicadas sang their evensong, a hummingbird stopped by her culinary window to flash its green luminosity before diving towards a nectared narcissus in her lush back garden.

'Octavio, Daddy will be home soon. Please bring your homework here for me to look at.' She called up to Octavio who was lost in a Grand Theft Auto game he'd taken to school that day, despite it being very much against the rules. He'd needed some ammunition for taunting in schoolyard wars. Rules were for Argentinean soccer players.

'Ok, Mama,' Octavio replied on command. He would have to lift another decent excuse from the crevices of his resourceful mind.   Homework in the life of young Octavio held little importance. He didn't see the value of focus in school at all. His Mama and Papa reassured him that all the riches Heaven could allow would be his on graduation day. While his parents tried to encourage scholastic endeavour, as a family, they knew he wouldn't need to rely on intellect once he was grown. The tacit knowledge fed his undernourished motivation. Octavio opted for manipulating others at recess as his main priority, rather than keeping his head in the books. So many gains could be made by keeping his power in tact and obtaining pesos or toys others had in their possession as ransom for their playground safety. He loved to score, perhaps innate to his birthright as Juan's son. Indeed, Octavio was corrupt. It might be said that he and his Papa were influenced equally by the manner in which many of the politicians ran the country.

Anyway, Octavio knew damn well his father had a massive fist in financing the very private school he went to. What did he need to obey moronic rules for?

Elisa continued on, checking the traditional Mexican rice with tomato, corn and peppers, and then moving onto salad prep. She served dinner in their home a little earlier than in most Mexican homes. In most families throughout the land of the agave, it was traditional to serve the ceña between 8:30 pm and 11 pm, once the heat of the day had subsided and the work was all done.

Juan, however, needed serious nourishment after his runs to Sinaloa or Tepic. That day, he was returning form a 3-day stint up to Juarez and would need some solid home cooking to counteract the adrenaline he'd been running on for over 72 hours. Octavio was coming out of a childhood growth spurt and he, too, seemed to have an endless appetite lately. So, they ate at closer to 7 pm in order that all should be contented.

She could hear Juan's navy Land Rover stealth in their driveway, the engine click off.

'Octavio! You must wash your hands and be ready for your Papa. Dinner is served.' Elisa called up to the boy.

Juan entered: a calm panther in his domicile. He went over to Elisa right away and took her in his arms from behind her perfect *nalgas*, where she was at the stove turning the rice off, about to check the roasting enchiladas. He was transfixed, relieved and, pleasured at the site of his beauty queen, the food he'd come home for, the lovely sunlight diminishing, all the aromas mixing with the fragrance of the fresh local flora from their dining room.

'Mmm-m, mi bella, mi reina.' Juan whispered in her ear as he slipped his left hand under one of her perfect buttocks. Elisa giggled, feeling a sudden rush of yearning below her belt buckle as a blush rose on her face. How she loved the return of her man. She elbowed him slightly, an attempt at keeping her own. The food needed attention and she couldn't go forward with her wishes in front of Octavio, who had bounded down the stairs to see Papa by this time.

'Papa, are you back for a while this time? Where did you go?' his son asked.

Elisa ushered her men to the table to continue talking. She went ahead and served her men, even opening their napkins on their laps for them. It is tradition that the women in Mexico serve the men. Still, to this very day, a grown man will not prepare his own food in his mother's home. She will always serve her man, wives and mothers, caretakers of the male. This is not disputed, except by those who have the advantage of being born in developed nations, with the secondary and pivotal advantage of being educated to think critically. Feminism has not yet taken root in Mexico, even in 2009. It is not a land hospitable to change and certainly not to progress organized in the matrilineal sense. It is what it is.

Elisa would throw caution to the wind every time if she felt it was merited, but she would not back out of the customs of being a Mexican woman. There was a line she would not cross. Her men were her treasures and she would not have either one raise a finger for himself when it came to food in her home. She saw it as part of the presentation of the meal. It was a matter of Pride.

'I am returning from an area in the northeast of our country, Octavio. This area is quite industrial, many people working hard', Juan replied, sipping cool purified water on ice with mint leaves. He was careful with his boy, his family. He treated his profession with dignity and the respect it deserved from one so enmeshed. Certainly, if a man is to make a living working inside a country-wide drug cartel, the understanding is that it is an *important* job, a veritable Service to the country. There is an understanding that the country itself could not exist without the infrastructure of 'bad money'.

The developing world doesn't stand a chance as a part of the developed world without some back up. This is how Juan validated his own difficult choices he faced each day in his motherland. The family lived in the elbow of drug-trafficking in Mexico: Guadalajara. It was inescapable. The bus driver, the police man, the store owner, the restaurateur: each had their daily business and an equally *rico* (rich) foil for it. The business would not move accordingly without the other business. Mexico sang out in a deep chocolate baritone, 'Let's be real here people. Keep it real.' The edifice was almost believable, latent beside the reality.

This was reality. Far from the Disneyland front painted by Puerto Vallarta or the hammocks swinging in poverty-ridden beachside Oaxaca was this: Reality. Know by its citizens who kept the superficial glitter up for margarita-sipping sweeties in from chilly Connecticut for a nice holiday.

Anyone could be a potential sale, personal or national politics aside. Far from the multi-layered filigree that is Mexico's beautiful, fragmented history, there is the base need for money.

The entire country was still lawless, uninsured. It was not subject to the same international codes of conduct as Europe or North America. Accountability is not a concept embraced to any degree in Mexico. It *cannot* be. In fact, Mexico has been seen as a playground for lawmakers of many demeanors. Mexico holds a conglomerate than is left unspoken, with a hoarse whisper of, 'I know. Yet I am beholden.' Juan's income, the *dinero* that fed his family, depended on her quietude as much as her helplessness.

'Papa, will you take me to play soccer in the park later, after dinner?' Octavio asked, sliding a steamy enchilada and rice into his mouth.

'No, no, mi niño. Not tonight. I am tired from the journey and all the hours of work over the last few days. Let's play tomorrow, after orange juice and chilaquiles for breakfast', Juan smiled evenly at Octavio. Manipulation had been this child's gripe water. His Papa knew how to manage it. He would not let it get to drama and personal assault.

'Papa, you *always* say this and I *always* miss you so much, you are gone so long. Why do I have to wait for my father?' There is nothing that hurts more than hearing the word 'no' when you have been away for someone for longer than you want to be.

Juan was ready for the backhand, lobbed high at neck level. 'I *know* and you *know* that we *know* we all love one another very much in this family, mi Precioso,' Juan said this emphatically, taking his boy's hands in his with each 'know' and looking into Octavio's hopeful eyes. 'You will *always* be my one and only Octavio. And there will *always* be soccer.' Juan was ultrasmooth, entirely unfretted by his son's clear show of Love, a hint of pressing Guilt served cold, on the side.

They lived in drama, they lived *for* drama. It was Juan's fatherly duty not to allow himself to *become* the Drama. To be an Osegura Vazquez meant to express. Juan had anticipated this from Octavio. The response script had been perfected hours before on the long road home.

'There will always be soccer, *para seguro*! And I will score on you like a madman tomorrow then, Papa!' Octavio exclaimed. Once Juan made his come back, Octavio already knew to retreat without contest. A little dig on Papa was in order, though.

His father was a strong man, a kind man, fair to his loved ones. But it was not wise to push him too hard. While Octavio didn't know the details and was too young for them to be relevant, he knew as much as when to accept his father's need for calm and space.

This acceptance fueled Octavio's playground skirmishes. It was too much to ask. The child knew something was happening, but he couldn't be sure what it was. As a result, he felt rejected to a degree. It is not easy to ask and not get as a child of privilege. Octavio accepted what he had to but he missed his Papa. He longed for a playmate of equal value and that is what his father embodied. He wondered every time his Papa left how long it would be before he could return. Or if he would return at all. There was an air of mystery surrounding his father. So much would be left unknown until Octavio was strong enough, old enough to hear the Truth. Juan had no choice but to protect Octavio by revealing nothing.

Octavio thought the world of his Papa, as so many young people do. He adored the man. Juan's limitations could not be revealed to such an impressionable young person. Elisa and Juan were raising the child the best they knew how and trying as hard as they could to shelter their boy from seeing Truth.

Juan was in no position to be transparent about his life with anyone, let alone a young child. His son was a feisty young boy and could slip up with his words at any time. This, in turn, could have catastrophic repercussions that might be felt as far away as the night clubs in Italy, or as close to home as the Texas senator's Friday night out with the boys. The maelstrom might even involve the same kind of gruesome bloodshed that had taken Pablo with his loose lips, or Pedro, with his disgruntled mistress. No one could be trusted. It was par for the course, part of the profession. There was no margin for error in a Narco family.

The border towns of Mexico, indeed, all of Mexico lately, was so frequently in international news, everyone was aware.

Some time ago, when they were least expecting it, and neither could shake it, Elisa and Juan had fallen in love. It was magical and languishing and ravenous, their love. Octavio was the most natural offspring of such a Love. The early courting lasted for days, they relished in one another. Juan had his first taste of riches and he had plenty time to be with his young Elisa. She was a jewel of a creature, a teenage doll, with the sassy edge of a strong young woman. Cool, tall, vulnerable Elisa. Verdant and guarded, she had been a mere 17 years old, he 26. Famished, he came in to Lulio, her workplace, to watch her arms move as she made lattes at the counter, delivered trays, waited on the chess-players in the front. He could not focus on anything else when she was there.

While Elisa's arms later grew to represent many shades of reciprocity to Juan, theirs was a love of verbal contracts. It was understood that agreements and taciturn observations preceded pragmatic judgment calls in each of the daily goings-on. They lived a selective reality. Each move was pre-thought and double-checked.

She felt safe, he felt like a hero. It worked in the deepest sense of Love. It worked for them, it kept them bonded. They had loved one another for some years. He still felt his heart skip and his pants tighten when she undulated past him. She still cared to ask if he needed a *limonada*.

Clearly, at that post-run moment he needed a shot of Jose Cuervo and a back massage.

'I want to go watch The Simpsons before bed.' He said it with the accent on the 'i', in the linguistic overlap of Spanish to English so that it came out more like 'S*ee*mpsons'. Juan nodded, longing for peace of mind, not blind to Octavio's attention-seeking.

'Off you go then!' Juan waved the air after Octavio, ready for more time with Elisa, perhaps sleep soon.

With that, Octavio was off, running up the stairs to his little boy's den, replete with a Play Station, his own telephone and more toys than would fill the bedrooms of three children. He pushed the peach stone of Loneliness that formed in his throat down as he picked up a play guitar.

These missions took all his energy. The anxiety was so high, even a shot of tequila would only scratch the surface. Every mission Juan wondered if he would make it, who along the line might slip in the internal chain of secrets. How he needed his woman's arms and her tenderness. Sleep deprivation and nerves on high alert for almost a week, after a particularly gruesome front-of-the-newspaper death scene related to his cartel had left Juan with no more reserves.

She knew. She went to their bedroom, her lithe frame calmed and comforted by his homecoming, her bare feet cooled by the marble floor. She prepared their bed for her husband, telling him she needed a moment, and asking him to relax on the bed. She went to the bathroom, where she had stashed her purse. Juan didn't need any more trouble on his mind. She took out the revolver carefully she had used in the salon earlier that day and laid it under their plushy towel pile. This was where she and Juan kept it hidden, amidst fresh-scented, Sofia-washed white *toalas* in the upstairs bathroom adjoining the master bedroom.

The proud front she kept for her bond with Juan meant he would not be privy to any part of the incident on that windy Tuesday at Frida's hair salon in Providencia. She slipped her arms around her man, relieved he was back again.

* * * * * * *

Chapter 4

Leer

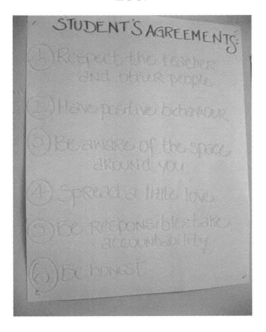

We artists are indestructible.

Even in a prison cell or a concentration camp,

I would be almighty in my own world of art.

Even if I had to paint my pictures with my wet tongue on the dusty floor of my cell.'

-Pablo Picasso

Gustavo was in the process of teaching himself to read. Every day, he made it his mission to obtain a newspaper by whatever means he could. He had most success walking into hotel lobbies and picking up a discard from a patron's breakfast time. He sounded out words and matched them to pictures. He sat near groups of men, taking a break for a Coke. He listened to their conversations about life and politics and the news. Gustavo was a small walking cerebral sponge.

Each day, he busied himself with words, fragments, spellings, revisions of spellings and pronunciations. He was always on the aware for new words or phrases to explain things. Gustavo became a word keener. He would have done anything to get more education, particularly in the Spanish language. It was as much work, the learning, as it was scrounging for food. His days were full, always on the run, yet he was never satisfied at the end of each day. He went to bed in hovel, often hungry, every time insatiate.

Gustavo, indeed, no Mexican citizens, could escape the rivers of blood the country was swimming in. Each day, a seemingly more gruesome image greeted him in print or out plain as day on the streets of Guadalajara. Scenes of the like smattered the whole nation, most concentrated in the towns in the North of Mexico, along the border into the US like Tijuana and Nogales. Glaring from the front cover, another slaying that was evidently Narco-related.

Gustavo began his pillaging around 9 am each day. Even when he felt victorious upon a newspaper free score, he felt equally sick looking at the front page. Today, the victim, unable to pay up on a coke debt, had both his hands shot out in the center, as well as 7 bullet wounds in the chest. His throat was sliced, almost in half, just enough to leave his head dangling in a morose manner. Gustavo wondered who has the gumption to take such intense photographs. He wondered if the photographer was paid well to walk in the center of the crime and capture it raw.

Tiny Gustavo felt a wave of nausea descend his torso, wriggling into the base of his throat and down within his guts as it serpented his insides. It read 'Narco Traficante, Juarez Run Goes South' in Spanish. The article went on to describe a midnight seizure-turned-massacre, led by the man pictured's inability to come up with the full amount of cash he owed for the drugs. The pictures were like this each day. It was unclear as to whether the killing was accomplished via the neck slice or the 7 bullet holes he had taken in the chest, but either way, the perpetrator was having a gratuitously violent Friday night out on the town. Gustavo was trying to unscramble the word 'Sur' for south in the Spanish headline.

It was not enough to put voice to, 'Pay up, now it's too late', via death. The opposing mafia had to add insult injury by underlining the fool's vital 'choice' to be murdered in full detail, a visual legacy of failure and lack left in the family of the deceased. And this was always the way: death, served up straight alongside shame, blame, guilt…a life sentence of the fouling kind. A message for future generations of that strain of the Paredes-Lopez family, the receiver of fate in this case.

Catholicism had etched itself and its punitive measures for failing to deliver into even the most hardened criminals in Mexico, reinterpreted. As such, the cost for messing up in the black market had to involve utter diminishing of the fool who snorted too much of the loot to be able to pay, or who had simply missed a pivotal connection.

Gustavo was sensitive to the ideas that he was putting together. He had no idea that other forms of media might be limited or exaggerated as the case may be. He had nothing to compare his life experiences to, except what he saw in 'La Journada' when he managed to salvage it. All he knew was that dangerous things happened in and near the city he called home. Below him, out on the streets, things he had best beware of were going on around him. It was the kind of landscape that required a tiny boy's eyes kept open wide, making it hard for him to sleep through a whole night. Many times, gunshots rang through the 2 am sky, scaring him yet again, awaking him from fitful sleeps. Often, he shivered in his sleep, no bed, only part of a blanket.

Gustavo had been born scared. It was almost as though fear was turning him to stone as he grew. He had not known a life free of it, so it was accepted to his inner being.

He used his fast intellect, combined with a refined sense of street wisdom and a dash of healthy mistrust to guide him. Gustavo was a pro at flying under the radar. He used his skills for survival and knew the value of keeping a low profile in order to see another day of street life. How he ached for a family. He held the dream alive that somewhere, there was a family for him. Perhaps he would be united with his people if he kept Hope alive. And so he did.

He kept a tiny space for Hope in his tiny heart and that is what motivated young Gustavo to keep moving on. Someday, someday.

He learned to read because he couldn't stop with words. Despite screaming evidence of malnutrition, his brain was very lively. His skin was raw in places, his growth perhaps stunted, though he had no comparison of sorts, as he wasn't quite sure how old he was. His belly was empty and distended with the imbalance of corrosive bacteria inside.

Loteria was one of his favourite tools for word acquisition, as it allowed him to draw correlations between the pictures of items he saw and the corresponding names of them on the cards. Gustavo loved the rare times that Ana Lisa had a moment to play with him, helping him with pronunciation, though she had no designs on vocabulary expansion herself. She was content to remain a basic linguist, while Gustavo aimed at someday becoming a champion of Scrabble. Ana Lisa had lost Hope some time back and had little room for games. She was content to use the dainty visuals of her ripe body for majority of her communication; the talks she had with Gustavo did not quite propel either child to deep levels of Socratian theory.

Gustavo was a perfectionist. He would learn it and play with it until it was no longer a question in his mind. He learned in order to solidify. Gustavo would become master or he would not attempt. This was innate to the boy. No matter what transpired in the life he trudged through, he had this refined sense. It had not been lost. Ana Lisa told him he was a *Milagro* (miracle).

The graphic descriptions Gustavo saw in each daily morsel of print he could muster set his brain in motion. Every day, he was increasingly curious about the state of the nation, the imminent drama of it all burned into his irises, deep etchings of awareness laid into the edges. He had deep circles of luminous black in the edges of them, closing out the edges classic brown colour, the colour of most Mexican eyes. These, the darkened outer nerve lines in Gustavo's, a sign of trouble early on in life.

Gustavo was becoming one of the best-informed young men in the land; equally consumed by his own growing verbosity. He stood to go to Ana Lisa, the rumble of hunger before him, the thought of how to ply money or food fresh in his mind. He turned towards the setting sun casting its *oro* shadow on the square outside the theatre in Centro.

* * * * * *

Maya had wanted two things as long as she could remember: to be a teacher and to live in Mexico. She had enjoyed her college time, and was ready to embrace education full-on now she had graduated a trained teacher. She had been raised near Beverly Hills, a fortunate child of a good Jewish family of wealth and vision. Maya had finished her training 3 years earlier at UCLA and had been teaching in the southwestern part of the San Gabriel valley in an eastern suburb of L.A. called Montebello. It housed majority blacks and Latinos; the workers of the US. Some were the legally building their lives, many were not. She wanted to add a little more cultural and lingual understanding to her teaching career. Maya felt her life of privilege could be dispersed by her and shared with the people of her country who struggled to make good on life.

Now, she had another opportunity and had taken it. She would go to Mexico to share her talents. She had left her boyfriend, Zach, her family and her previous 3rd grade teaching position to go to Guadalajara, Mexico, to teach its more privileged children ESL. She had applied, got the job in a day, and within a month, she was off, bag in hand.

Maya had not learned everything she could have while she was in high school Spanish. She had a teenage habit of skipping school to go find Theo, her then-boyfriend. It was more interesting to the young Maya to kiss Theo at the end of parking lot five than it was to attend class when she was 16. Maya could always understand the school-skippers, the rebels and the irreverent kids. In fact, she liked the underdogs, as she, too, had not had much of a taste for The System in her youth. Maya was gorgeous, luscious and healthy. She enjoyed large breasts, the envy of her girlfriends, which caused many a young male admirer to salivate over her.   The boys called Maya, 'juicy'.

She was an angel to most eyes. She had a strong, sweet nature and a keen intellect, a tender heart. She was a popular one wherever she went.   Her career plan had been well thought out. She knew she'd have to expand her use of the language beyond the basics in order to have some kind of life in Mexico. She would make a life there, in the hot sun, the authenticity of its landscape and history would be her next study.

She arrived in late June, ready to begin teaching at the end of July. This gave her enough time to find a place to live and to begin to forge trust with her neighbours in her Colonia, Mezquitan Country, near Templo San Bernardo, off Plan de San Luis. It was so named, as Mesquite trees lined the funky pavements near the graveyard, 5 blocks from her apartment.

Rosa, next door, had greeted her with a sack of fresh-grown tomatoes. Maya was revered immediately. Her neighbours became her friends. They all asked what her religion was, if she had a husband and children and what her bloodline was. They were very keen to understand her ancestry and share anthropology, offering up stories of their own. Some had Aztec blood; some families had lived in Guadalajara for centuries.

They were also quick to share any illness, injury or family drama. Elena's son had recovered from Heroin addiction, but she was always worried for him. Monica, across the street was so frustrated with her husband; she hit him in public, causing her children to wail often. (Monica was the least favourite in the neighbourhood. She confided in Maya she had mental health issues on their second day of acquaintance. Maya felt more sympathy, less judgment towards this sad woman). Rosa struggled with edema and arthritis from years of consuming too much starch, animal fat and salt. Cesar, up the road, had lost his girlfriend in a highway accident about a month earlier and was grieving as he fixed cars in his driveway, the Colonia's revered mechanic. Maya felt the rawness of their lives and was interested to note how willingly they wanted to share, making a bridge of their internal lives to hers. There was no pretense here; no one tried to hide their losses or cover with a brave face.

And they always stopped to talk. Maya could not hurry past, as she might have in L.A. She would have appeared very rude if she had not made time to stop and chat with everyone. She realized this early on and got into the habit of leaving home 15 minutes earlier than she needed to in order to accommodate conversation.

Each weekend, Maya took the half-built subway (yet to be completed) or walked to a different part of the city. She had recently become stuck on Centro, with its slew of yummy things to eat and good deals. There was a lot of action in Centro, often a protest or a speech being given, an art display to wander through or young people with *trens* (dreadlocks) drumming near Juarez station. She liked to head down to watch the people and enjoy new ice cream flavours on a Saturday. There was lots of opportunity to practice her Spanish there. As well, it gave her a view into authentic life in Mexico outside the U.S.-influenced modern fabrication of resort cities like Acapulco or Cancun.

She saw the U.S. impact everywhere, from trends to rebellion, to the political and rather radical views of the young beatniks who chanted about Mexico 'becoming her own woman' again, free of U.S. influence and control. Sure, the U.S. was hated my many, especially the educated, but it was also revered for its Hollywood, its music, its styles, its food options. They seemed to spout a love-hate mix of drivel, dancing to the Black Eyed Peas or Usher while sipping Coronas in huddled teenage groups near cars, all the while touting internal fire that sang a verdant chorus of, 'We are Mexican, we are not yours to take!'

Beads for making necklaces, music at a 15% discount for teachers, computer parts, art supplies, racy underwear for the equivalent $1.50 a pair or less-it was all there, in the bustling stalls of San Juan de Dios, alongside candles to burn in remembrance of the dead and love potions to cast when the time is right.

Maya took in everything. At times, she would sit down, half a bag of coconut water in hand, a rest there amidst the busy-ness. Even watching took all her energy. This was colour in Kodachrome. This was better than any video she could rent; it became her study and her entertainment.

She looked at colours, smelled spicy food cooking, glanced at beautiful strangers; she shopped with a handful of pesos and still came out with armloads of goods and change. It was exactly what she had imagined and much more, this amazingly festive life in Mexico. The longer she stayed, the deeper the story, the richness of the country's long bloody history became to her. Understanding was growing.

As Maya began her ascent up the stairs to a peppers stall at San Juan de Dios, a small child pulled at the length of her blue trench.

'Hola y buenos tarde, Señorita. No tengo dinero para comidas y-' Gustavo started. ('Hello and good afternoon, young lady. I have no money for food and-')

Maya pulled 100 pesos out of her pocket, the equivalent of about $12 U.S., without question, not allowing the child to finish. She had saved at least that much in her deal-spotting downtown today. How this little street urchin moved her! What eyes he had! She could read in an instant his horrific circumstance. A man at a DVD/CD stall across the way spotted dinero and attempted to distract her for a buy with a subtle turning up the volume on Kate Voegele's '99 Times' so that the tianguis stalls surrounding them were literally rocking.

This was more than the little orphan had ever seen at one time, the equivalent of about ten meals, real solid meals! His fear and frustration broke like a stream of sunlight after a Guadalajara monsoon.

Maya didn't need to know or hear any more. She blew an air kiss at him and went on her way. It was, somehow, simply too sad to linger on. 'Let him be happy in his own world for a moment before the money's spent', Maya thought.

She was gone, Gustavo was rich. He could not believe this miracle was his. He turned to go to Ana Lisa to share the news and buy her a fancy dinner. Esplendido!

As Gustavo turned, enshrouded in newfound mirth, such a rarity, the child sensed something else. It was cold, almost stainless steel sterile chilly.

He turned. He faced Bettos.

Bettos stared back, eyes locking with Gustavo's, hands open by his sides.

* * * * * * * *

Chapter 5

El Dolor, El Regalo

'God don't give us nothing we can't handle'

—Neil Young, interviewed circa 1999

Maya was moving through multiple emotions in those first few weeks of adjustment. It had been hard for her to leave Zach, the only definite hiccup in her departure from L.A. They were aiming to try to make things work despite the distance. He would keep his job in IT for a year and if things looked promising further south, he would look at joining her there in future.

Still, she felt his absence often in those first moments and pined for him relentlessly. She was not interested in taking up with anyone else, yet was too young to marry Zach. Her career would get all the focus it deserved without her man along to distract her. Still, the heart wants what it wants. She missed him every night, the bed felt empty and kind of stark in the mornings. There were many things she was discovering she would have liked for him to have experienced also. The music! The food! The crazy passionate antics in the streets! The utter freedom to suck face in public! Zach would have enjoyed all that.

She knew this was something she had promised herself. Zach had been very understanding about it. Their next visit had been planned for September, when she had a few days' break for Dia de Independencia. Things could be re-evaluated then if it proved too much. She had signed a contract with the school she was to work at for the entire school year, end of July to the following end of July, so she would be there over 13 months total. She was not one to renegue on her promises.

Maya decided she would keep a diary so help her stay balanced and to record the unparalleled things she was witnessing all the time. She never quite knew what would hit her as she walked out each day. She also decided to go to the Baratillo, a major blocks-long market where one could find most anything, for cheap. Her love of bargains led her to research how far on the subway she could travel to get off at the right place in the south eastern end of the city. She decided to subway there and then bike home after making the purchase of wheels. She would stop for ice cream and *durros* on the way home, her new favourite comfort foods. They had ice cream of flavours and varieties she had not seen at home. She might enjoy mangosteen again. It had been hard to contain herself the last time she had beat the heat at the end of June with the yummy Michoacán fresh made treat.

She wrote her first diary entry a few days after purchasing a small chrome trick bike at the market and getting into a slight mishap with it. She was already teaching adult ESL classes in Business Negotiations English at night, from 5 - 9 pm, and she was using her bike to get across town to the school. Who knew? Perhaps she would become a travel writer or publish a collection of short stories about Mexican life one day. She had always liked to write, especially if she felt lonely. Maya was gathering so many stories every day; she decided to get right on it. Her new bike and her journal became her road allies in her fight against missing Zach.

From Maya's diary, July 3/2009:

Serendipity

'As I was en route to teach an adult ESL night class at the Honda factory in nearby industrial Salto outside central Guadalajara, Mexico, I decided to stop at the bank and grab some money for fish tacos. Strange how if you carry an idea inside your head for long enough and it is strong enough, it begins to materialize, but maybe not so much in the way you'd expected. I was carrying a little need for Hope in humanity. Feeling a little low, a little out of my element.

I pulled my trick bike (chrome, styling, 500 pesos at the Baratillo) up to a lamp post outside the bank in Chapultepec, noticing only vaguely that I was situated on top of a manhole cover and that there existed a tiny gap, just under where I was standing. A gap just large enough to house sliding keys. A gap that, despite it's small space, seemed to have reaching power, a power beyond itself, the very power by which to grab my precarious keys and pull them deep into it's pedestrian walkway-housed lurking midst. And, so it happened: my house/bike/front gate keys took flight from the end of the chain and the key that unlocked my bike chain, took a graceful, rapid arc, and flew right on into The Sewer of Untreated Doom below. There they went the lot of them, fast as water, fast as a cockroach that senses heat, down into No Man's Land.

Fuck. I was in a hurry, as always. It seems like things in Mexico always take a long, long time. Lines go on forever, things take awhile. It sure is different from the harried pace in L.A.! I think it is due to the vast and booming populous in Guadalajara, but this might be coupled with my own lack of patience. At the moment the keys took flight, I felt a pulsating flash of anxiety in the realization that I had 3.43 minutes before I needed to get over to the school to take the 1-hour ride out to the factory to teach a 2.5 hour class in English to people who support the globalization of Honda cars at a Japanese-owned production plant where tardiness is pure villainy.

I scanned the area, sure my keys were lost, relieved mildly that I had thought to make a spare set. This particular key chain contained the tiny cat charm that Teresa had given me for my birthday two years back. My Batman the cat charm! It is *lucky*, that charm! I needed *those* keys. I needed to be a Princess about it. I was about to leave, suck it up, not say anything and push my Inner Princess down. But then I saw my glint of Hope. I saw The Outside Bank Security Guard: gun, heavy stick, uniform, leaded boots. Yup, he was my man. He was going to be My Hero.

This was not about sexuality, as I was clearly *not* attracted to this man. He was seriously unattractive to me, as are all men in uniforms, all the time. Cops and security guards to me represent a human repugnancy: the inability to follow one's own lead. To me, they seem juxtaposed as masculine mannequins, unable to think for themselves, with a special need to conform to ensure their *supposed* manliness. I like a maverick every time.

This was about needing a problem solved and finding the right man to help me out. This was me pulling the old Damsel in Distress card.

I had found a match!

I motioned for him to come over to me, as if this was His *Job*, and explained what had happened. My mangled Spanish actually worked when it needed to. I could literally *see* the machismo rising slowly in his veins. I could taste his altruism, moving forward from reptilian brain to cerebral cortex and sliding into first at the front-and-central portion of his forehead: *el lobo*. I could smell his manliness, beneath his Old Spice, his crispy hair gel, his chewing gum, and the slow smile that began to spread across his face. This man had A Purpose; his day could begin.

And he was game. Was he ever game! He took the barrel of his gun adeptly and tried to slide it down the small hole to capture the keys, and then pull them up. We could now both see the keys; they had fallen and lay, amazingly dry, about two feet down the hole. The hole was not filled with filthy muck, as I had assumed. It was clear and dry, but it was very slim.

Ok, they were salvageable. His ingrained machismo would prove to have Due Purpose if he could, in fact, save the day. He tried and he twisted and he pulled, to no avail. The barrel was slightly too large to scoop the key ring. The security guard drew himself up. He kept smiling, though. He wasn't letting his Great Wall down. He could not fail a Damsel really, not by unwritten Mexican Male Code. That would result is Shame beyond words on his part. I knew we were on side on the road to victory here. I *knew* it.

He looked around, checked the time. I checked the time. I needed to leave in 57 seconds. There was no way. I would be late. But, it was still worth the try. We were in it now. The security guard spotted a coat hanger on the street, outside the parkade, nearby the bank machine I had hoped to enter to withdraw money I had wanted in order to purchase fish tacos. He walked over to the coast hanger, picked it up and untwisted it. He then wrapped it around the barrel of his gun. He was going to be a mega *caballero* and make a special, perfect-sized scoop with which to get those keys. It was as though nothing else mattered to this man.

He tried again. He tried and he tried and he tried and he went out of his way to keep trying. Despite his kind heart, and his best efforts, there was no way these keys could be scooped with that contraption. We both looked at each other and sighed and smiled. Perseverance.

Then, we looked for help. He kept smiling. Optimism soared from his chest. He would not be moved to anything but the keys and the damsel. I was fascinated. I had never experienced this in the U.S. Most would have walked on by, leaving me to sort it out by myself, too 'busy' to assist.

By this time, I was late. I sent my ESL-teaching cohorts a text message to say I would be late. I couldn't give up now. I was locked into The Finding of The Keys. We scouted more help; this wasn't going to be easy. There was another security guard outside the bank, two *inside* the bank and one other parking arcade attendant. We motioned for them to come over. We really only motioned the other outside security guard, but everyone, all 4 other People With Uneventful Jobs came over anyway. There I was, in a swarm of guns, clubs, pheromones, tucked-in shirts, aftershave that reeked Sin; a single masked damsel, in a wealth of Men Who Had Machismo and Wanted to Help. Was I in Heaven or was I in Hell?

They went to work right away. Rapid discussion of the serious situation in Spanish ensued. There was laughing, talking, and many questions to be answered. The loss of the keys became The Event of The Day. An 'Alturas Securidad' truck pulled up. The man driving it got out, and stopped to get involved instead of going into the bank to see the manager about the upstairs system. Another man, with a suit and a brief case pulled up and double-parked. No one flinched, no one told him to move his vehicle. He got right into it instead of going to meet with the branch CEO about the New Mortgage Solution. A man I considered sexy walked by in a business suit, tripped on his untied shoelace, and then laughed at himself. As he picked himself up, the other Men made sure This Man, too, understood The Damsel's Plight. (Oh, he *was* sexy, an opportunity with no wedding band in sight, but I was masked and on-task and my shyness permeated me in concentration, so he never knew. In my head, I hid the naughty thought from Zach)

The other outside security guard took an oratory role, advising the pack of others what to do. The two inside security guards went to look for other things that might be used to pull the keys up and out. I now had 8 other people, Men, fully involved in The Finding of the Keys. There was nothing more important to these men than to help me.

But it was the dirty-jeans-clad parking attendant who was the ultimate victor, the most virile of the lot.

The parking lot attendant took his Long Stick. Of course, he just happened to have a long stick handy, as he was a parking arcade attendant. It was a veritable part of his tool kit. He then took a metal wire, also handy, wrapped it around the stick, creating a hook. He slowly, carefully dropped it down into the hole. He missed. He slowly, carefully dropped it down into the hole. He missed. He slowly, carefully dropped it down into the hole. He missed. He slowly, carefully dropped it down into the hole. He missed. He slowly, carefully dropped it down the hole and missed 11 times. On the 12th time, he swung it: he raised my keys very carefully up out of the hole, as the crowd watching, all of them thinking *they* really had the best method of key-removal possible up their male sleeves, raised their voices in a kind of a uniform scale.

Ah-ah-ah-ah-ah-ah-ah-aaaa-h!' they sang in a crescendo-ing wave of male voice. Parking Arcade Attendant raised those keys, right up straight across from my astonished eyes. He had done it: he'd pulled Hope out of nowhere!

I was now 7.32 minutes late. It, being Mexico, was of no concern and would be met with, 'De nada', and another requisite 20-minute wait anyway, once I arrived at the school to go to the factory.

It was a rare and beautiful synchronicity.

I grabbed my keys joyously. I made a very girly happy type of a noise. There I was standing, the epicenter of a circle of attendees, so utterly machismo, all of them. Large feet, underarm wetness, musky smell. We were united in victory for that moment. I had my keys and this man had done his job, had satisfied his instinct. I had been assisted in my moment of crisis. We beamed at one another, the late afternoon halcyon backlight dancing on our heads. It all seemed very slow motion. Strange, happy guttural noises emitted from the victorious men folk. They were united as men! It no longer mattered *which* man had done the deed. Male success had transpired, and so there had been produced a team camaraderie on this late Thursday afternoon. It mattered that the deed that was requireth of the Silly Damsel Fluffball Cutesy womankind had been achieved. It mattered that her *nalga* (butt) could be viewed in three dimensions as she biked away. They had each other's backs for the next roll of the dice. Bikegirl Roulette. X-Ray Eyes. Strip Poker.

Silly, girly giggles continued to be emitted from me. They seemed like male angels. It seemed like a fiesta. I dropped their obvious Male Agenda, bound in dark leather, in a wake of unmasked latitude that had emerged temporarily from my own immediate mirth.

We all laughed together, me ever-conscious of the time; they completely absorbed in the moment. Those men were Present. They were, indeed, steadfast. I hugged each reeking man, noting the Parking Arcade Attendant was the only man who did not stink to high heaven of many conflicting chemicals.   That afternoon in sunny Guadalajara, he was my hero: dressed in plain jeans and a t-shirt.

I thanked them all numerous times, still laughing through my Spanish, 'Muchos, *muchos* gracias! Gracias para tu ayudas! Gracias de Dios! Hasta luego! Te vaya bien! Gracias, mis hombres!' I hopped on my bike, keys in hand and biked away to teach at Honda.

They all stared at my *nalgas* (buttocks). I could feel it.'

Indeed, Maya's diary was taking on a voice of its own. Maya was beginning to see the value of transcendence and strength through her tears in her choice to be in Mexico this particular year.

* * * * * * *

Chapter 6
Amor

'Only love can stop your fear,

Only fear can stop your loving.'

–Morcheeba, from 'Love and Fear', circa 1997

Elisa's Love had come to her, walked right in and plucked her the very day she needed it most. While she worked hard, and was often beyond tired at the end of her shift at Lulio, she didn't have to work for requited love. Juan had seen her come running into work, a flurry of youthful golden sparkles and jasmine scent, as he sipped his unsweetened Americano. The year was 1997. Young Elisa was a mere teenager, all hormones, pimple concealer and hushed adrenaline. She darted across the street, on target, legs of a gazelle, even then. Juan was smitten.

Elisa had the smile of a deity. She didn't find it so easy to smile. She felt an urgent, slightly anxious, 'What happens *next*?' most of the time, youthful curiousity with a hint of anxiety. She had to work hard to smile because there seemed to be a lot to get through in her mind, so often preoccupied. And so when Elisa could be coaxed to smile, it spread across her lovely face slowly, then it opened, like a lotus flower, it blossomed into a sincere, kind of shared bond of affection. She had been known to make a random by passer's day if she was seen to be smiling, or better yet, laughing, boca wide open to the Heavens that gifted her so. Juan thought she looked a little like a teen Bebel Gilberto, his favourite Brazilian singer.

Juan could not stop himself. His glance quickly evaporated into a headful of amorous thoughts about this dear young girl. He was entranced by her pure freshness, pure vivacity. He sensed the Struggle to Smile was hers. Oh, she had a Story, just as we all do. The slip of anxiety that coursed her veins worked to churn the butter even more for him. He wanted a hand in this teen-woman's life; he wanted a piece of this one. It was a perfect chance for a Hero!

It amused him no end to come in each morning for his fresh-squeezed orange juice and his chilaquiles, preceded by a steaming strong Americano. Not only did Lulio make the best breakfast, his heart was tickled by this young beauty. He grew quite addicted to the young Elisa.

And so it was that they courted, a long slow steady flame. On it went. Juan went about devouring Elisa; she succumbed to his heroics. She couldn't hold back. Juan gave her a newfound sense of security, filled that void. He acted as though he had all the time in the world for her, smiling his sexy smile of adoration. Juan couldn't get enough of this little minx in her white half apron, making the lattes, sunlight in her bangs and her*pasilla* powder-coloured eyes. He loved the way she smelled like bubblegum and hair gel, baby powder and youth. Everything about Elisa bounced: her hair, shiny in a pony tail, her skirt, her bottom, she perky teenage breasts. Elisa: fresh, vibrant, full of life, some kind of promise of Hope for one who needed it most.

Juan's romantic heart overflowed; he loved her every nuance. He stopped by every day to admire her.

This did wonders for Elisa's self esteem. She had felt Forgotten for so long, even Invisible. Now here was this darkly handsome stranger come to smile at her and be nice. She pushed the hair out of her face, shifting her wad of gum to the other side of her mouth.

'Hola, Señor. Como estas?' she said gently to Juan, looking him right in the eye with her smile, the smile she saved just for Him.

He was paralyzed. He could only chuckle into his own grin, his nerves running on high. Everything about her was so entrancing. He laughed inwardly at his boyishness, outwardly at his lust.

'Bien, Gracias. Y tu?' he asked, unable to stop looking on her with such pure *amor* in his eyes. He felt the caffeine awaken his veins before it even hit his mouth. The lime in the bubbly water he drank beside it touched his lips to help him stave off being overwhelmed. In Elisa's presence, he was overcome with feeling, but he must not let her see.

'Ah si. Bien,' She was enamored, but could not let it her own Poker cards be glimpsed. Elisa made a coy, somewhat coltish movement of initiating the daily sweep of the front steps and the entrance to Lulio. Juan ogled her, as he simultaneously sipped his coffee. He looked at his compatriots being offed by the score in the gory reporting of the front page of the newspaper. It was all happening. Soft gentle feelings, coupled with hardened leathery ones.

Juan could not wait another morning for Elisa. He asked her for her phone number.

'I have no phone, Señor.'

'No phone? How can this be? You are *lost* without a phone!' Juan answered his dreamy little angel chica bella.

'I am too young. They will not give me one until I turn 18.' Elisa answered, as if it were of little consequence.

Juan gulped. She *was* young, this one.

'So, how much longer until you are 18?' he asked.

'8 and ½ months.' Elisa replied.

He finished his breakfast, checked his cell for messages.

'How can I see you then, if you have no phone?' he asked.

'I can meet you here after my shift ends at 3:30 pm.'

'3:30 it is. See you then.' Juan replied.

* * * * * *

Juan was on his way into another day of meet-ups, drop offs, essential calls and a meeting with The Boss and Bettos. They needed a Mule-and fast.

All he could think about was the charming Elisa.

He dodged traffic expertly, hummed along to Café Tacuba, 'Eres', imagining Elisa undressing. He whizzed past the 24-hour flower shop, adjacent to the cemetery. As he glanced at the open-faced lilies, all frosty pink, he thought of Elisa and her lip gloss. Her bubblegum smell, her teenage body. The imagery was resplendent to say the least.

Elisa crafted lattes all day, expertly multi-tasking, answering the phone, taking the customers food orders and delivering with style. Every day of work, her sense of Self grew slightly. She became 'somebody' at Lulio. The convergent mix of artists, writers, readers, businesspeople, chess-players, all humming a subconscious symphony inside an ancient monk's cellar, nee library, nee Lulio, the popular gathering place. The food was excellent, the service, some of the best. It was fluid intellectual community, the meal of the day.

The job suited Elisa; her days flew by. She loved to get dressed up in her pretty best and give the people what they wanted. She tried her best to avoid thoughts of Juan; her impetus being survival. Love had seen her get her share in the past. She didn't want to hook her hopes on anything that might not last. Life had not given Elisa much substance on which to build. She was loathe to lose anything that she had inside, for Elisa had a loyal heart and once she gave it, she knew she would not move from that.

She didn't want to get taken for another ride, as she had felt she'd been in her birth family. It was more instinct, but she greeted Juan's affections with a deserving skepticism. While she loved the attention, she didn't trust him yet.

She walked the line between the fear of loss and the need for adoration.

* * * * * * *

The traffic kicked up dust, drivers were impatient, honking. The coffees flowed in an unending stream, the human chatter babbling along with the live music of street musicians. Her day closed in as 3:30 pm approached.

Juan stopped to pick up a bunch of pink roses for Elisa.

He walked to the front of the restaurant, past Domingo, with his nose and ear hairs sprouting everywhere, with the *floras* in hand and looked at her. She looked up from an order going in to the chef. As she turned to look, Elisa felt Aphrodite's electric greeting even before Juan said hello.

* * * * * * *

Chapter 7

Movemiento y Cambiando

If you got bad news
You want to kick them blues
Cocaine.
When your day is done and you wanna ride on
Cocaine.
She don't lie
She don't lie
She don't lie
Cocaine'

J.J. Cale, from 'Cocaine', 1976

On her way to school that morning, at 7:13 am, Maya was listening to The Arcade Fire, full volume and trying to keep her waning spirits from heeding the call of the gutter. She was trying to think of ways her brother had made her laugh as a child.

At 7:15 am, further along her route that morning, Maya was affronted with a man who pulled his large red truck over at the corner. He got out, 3/4 of a block ahead of her, and stood, with the driver's side door open. This hefty man, in a grey stained t-shirt, and fat-boy jeans felt that very minute was an appropriate time to begin masturbating. He jacked off; penis exposed to the dusty wind, while his truck blared atrociously loud, fast *Banda* music. Once he was finished, he looked right at Maya. She was trying to cross the street hurriedly once she realized what he was doing.

He continued to seek her eyes. Then, he smiled, a slow, grease ball smirk as she tried frantically to look away.

He roared off in his truck.

Was he *laughing*?

* * * * * * * *

Metamorphosis, a scientific change, is described as, *'a variation in biological development; a variance in the pattern of development of an organism as a result of changes in the external environment.'* The only reasonable explanation as to how cocaine became the world's biggest rocket fuel can be likened to the scientific explanation of metamorphosis.

The drug takes quite a journey to get across world borders. Once it hits the borders, the rapid-souring ride only continues.

Legislation to control cocaine was attempted; politicians, most of them snorting the very stuff they push to control, ban or serve life sentences for trafficking have tried to calm its incessant and now heightened heartbeat.

Reagan thought in the most earnest and Manifest Destiny of ways he was bringing America justice, liberation from the coke epidemic, when he and dear Nancy went in heavy on the Anti Drug movement from 1981 to 1989. Some would say the gravest damage had already been done. Addiction of the masses had already transpired Big Time. Hell, even Mister Rogers was hooked.

This is always the best time to levy taxes or fines or imprison: beat 'em when they're already down.

The thing is, like rats in a cage moving particulate diseases, both cocaine addicts and those who enjoy it socially for fun on weekends alike will do what needs to be done to keep the world's favourite white powder moving. More money will be borrowed or earned-legitimately or otherwise.

Coke rules the rulers. It moves so much cash, it's bigger than the law. Even U.S. Law.

It is astonishing that a tiny seed can grow into the world's biggest underground black market economy. So prevalent is cocaine now that it appears to be relatively central on many agendas, both actively political and those more taciturn. Acceptance has arrived ultimately in the team coach of Heavy Use.

"Can't beat 'em? Join 'em" could be one way the subject is looked upon in terms of conspiracy. Conspiracy loves controversy, so the two are already in bed together. Couple that with the world at large's inability to stay non-addicted with the vast love of sex…and you have it: this is one drug that cannot be put down. Sure, it offers about 20 minutes of fun and then drains the bank account in one good night. But cokeheads still can't get enough.

Coke is not even seen as sleazy or wild or naughty any more. It's a part of an average Friday night out in New York City for a group of hairstylists after work. It's a part of hospital deliveries that come and go all day long at a given private hospital outside Santa Monica. It's the catalyst for fun across the board all over the world at this point. From tiny farms in the Midwest to kids up north in Vancouver to play for the weekend- it is *everywhere;* it's demand incessant. Despite multiple discussions worldwide, legislation with penalties, education, the yayo still holds widespread appeal.

Those who chose not to participate are practically the minority.

The cocoa plant seed has all the life force removed from it: refined, purified, sold, non-purified, cut, handled, cut again, managed, moved and snorted. And yet it stays so vital, produces so easily and abundantly, the power the seed holds can survive. Despite the myriad routes it travels in metamorphosis, Power is the very thing that keeps its hold so strong.

Power. Now there's one thing people the world over can't get enough of.

And for 20 minutes, for the fool who is vacuous enough in spirit to believe coke's blinding, soul-defying message, Power is theirs. The sexy velveteen of Power. Imagine, if you've never felt powerful what a drug like that does for you.

While cocaine may hit the border at Tijuana in a white powdered form, closest to its truest nature, it will not stay as such. It will be bastardized almost immediately. This is mostly due to the rising price of the drug, as well as the random the difficulties faced in supplying it. It can be cut with something as innocuous as baking soda. A cheap cut is used, with no regard for the long-term or poisoning effect on the consumer. It can alternately be mixed with rat poison. Seeing as there is no insurance on the street drug, this cutting process cannot be monitored. The buyer doesn't know what they're getting. If they are one of many who become addicts, they don't rightly know what they're addicted to.

Many wonder what is wrong with them as their poisoned insides rot.

A Coker is as much of a crack head as the next guy. Some dress up fancy and eat out most nights. Others are jonesing in last week's puke-stained jeans on the sidewalks of East Vancouver, BC, scrounging about for even a spec of it. They're all in the same boast, drawn down the river by the same captain. The people *seem* different, but the vein of commonality between them is like-minded. They are all in need.

They act like they don't know each other and it seems from the outside like they don't. Did that Canadian Hockey star with a bank roll of well over 7 million really walk the same streets as the lowest of the low to get that high? Yup. Because that's where the Pharmacy is, dude: in the most villainous, disgusting human sewers of the world. They're both serving the same God, both running as fast as their hungry appetites will carry them for the same feeling.

Vancouver, BC is a classic case in point, one known and studied world-wide. A lot of snow moves into the city via boat or land. It takes a trip through Crack Alley and the Downtown Eastside. Usually, the need to make money necessitates the cutting of the pure drug with other powder(s).

It moves around, hand to hand, until an 8-ball finds its way into an unemployed tree planters' hands at the end of the high-output bush season, or hits the mitts of a stockbroker at the end of a long market day. Doctors, lawyers, sports heroes, politicians, they may well have red nostrils at the end of the night. Strippers, hookers, pimps, they may be just as keen. It's the one universal pace everyone can go for 20 minutes of oblivion, more time spent there if you got the money.

* * * * * * * *

It is very human and very understandable to seek debauchery sometimes. Who doesn't desire a shade of oblivion once in a while? The real irony is at the beginning, the user is the life of the party. By the time addiction has set in, the very same shell of a person remains, but not so much what they were, now hiding away in 7-Eleven bathrooms to get their fix. They feel anything but social at that point.

It's not about good and bad. It is what it is. It's about what gets people through. It doesn't hurt so much going up. It hurts like Hell on the way back down. Hence, the very real need for more. More more more. For the few moments a person is up, they're down for a day or more.

It takes awhile for the coke molecule to leave the system. Each line elongates the coming down process. The effect doesn't stop after one night. One line of Cocaine adheres to the motility of sperm, affecting its movement for up to 5 full years after it's been used. The menstrual cycle in women can be altered with the ingestion of a single rail. Over time, infertility, preceded by in males the inability to get it up, is unavoidable.

Where cocaine was enjoyed socially through the 20's, 30's, 40's and 50's, it took a minor detour when it was eclipsed by LSD during the 60's. Coke, the hometown hero rode in again in shiny new boots during the 70's and the 80's. It came back better than ever, stronger and more popular. It has seen a revitalization of sorts since about 1997, particularly through America, North America and throughout Europe. These places have enough affluence to get it, even in its rough-hewn cut copy form.

Ironic that a person could afford a maid to clean their home, but would allow their intestinal fortitude to be so compromised, their immune system so abolished with each rail snorted. The inside of the person wasting to a derelict state, but the house still looks great.

It's a great drug for those who live in deluded forms of reality as all it does is reinforce paranoid delusion. It takes dreams and tours them into nightmares.

No, the movement of cocaine isn't changing, but the way it addicts is. The numbers who have access to it is changing.

The numbers who try, then like, then want, then need are growing.

The numbers who willingly? Drunkenly? Suicidally? ingest a filthy impure mini-high. The human home, left a mess.

To feel loved. Adored. Cherished. Powerful.

Even for 20 minutes.

Isn't that what parents do for a child when he or she is first born? Isn't that what being held tight feels like?

Les we forget how many were never held tight. How many *don't* know anything but coke's power hold. Coke doesn't love unconditionally; it takes a vice grip. Its death road slow but steady.

If it fails to kill the person, it surely kills the sprit, which takes very little time.

If coke fails to kill the person, it kills the spirit, which takes very little time.

When coke is cut with baking soda, it can be cooked up into poor cousin Crack. This is where the drug gets heavy. Crack scars litter the Downtown Eastside back to the case in point. No mention need be made of the countless other Under the Bridge zones that are causing renal failure, paralysis, nerve damage, intestinal issues, sexual impotence, headaches, fever, nausea, immune system destruction, and teeth-grinding before Death climbs aboard to kill first the true sprit and soul, then the entire person.

It claims lives of the most prestigious, at the same time as it hooks the most vulnerable: street dwellers that have no other life. It is smoked; the high lasts even less time than the full tilt achieved on lines which are snorted. It must be smoked again-and fast. We can see the addicted jonesing for their Crack out on the street. We can see the affluent breaking dates, leaving gatherings early and lying at work or to loved ones. To get It. POWER.

Metamorphosis, '*a variation in biological development; a variance in the pattern of development of an organism as a result of changes in the external environment.*' The drug, a part of the external environment, is introduced to the organic system more frequently as needed. This causes internal and irreversible changes in the organic being. The once-upright member of humanity is reduced to a crawling wrecker, a soon-to-be meal for maggots.

How then does the metamorphosis of cocaine use differ from person to person, from social class to social class? It doesn't: The Great Leveler. In the end, the addict is no better than a common street rat. It is the most communist of all drugs, the biggest purveyor of ostentation-ruination.

Power. It's blinding white light seductive and sweet, it punishes every time.

Yes, it is very effective at attaining loss of Life, this devil drug. The only ones who have control over Coke, are the ones who have limited access to its supply. Where it is available readily, it is knocking people down, stealing dreams and lives insidiously along the way. When does a person know their life has been stolen by Coke? Once it's gone.

Some horrifying changes in personality happen along the way, of course. The human body *knows* it is enduring poison. It *knows* it is under false pretense. It *knows* deep inside it is fully powerless, to the drug- and likely an impotent soul in the grand understanding of Life.

Know any Cokehead that is held in high regard? Usually, they can find others to Coke it up with, certainly. But the general feeling towards the Cokey person is major lack of Trust. The coke head feels Powerful but is, in fact, viewed with no respect. Yes, even by the ones using alongside.

There's more irony.

The rivulet spans that coke takes on its ravenous ride are like grimy little fingers across grand nations. It is a disease.

One of the major rivers in Italy, the Po, has been reported to be a cess pool of residual cocaine (pub. 2007, Globe and Mail, Canada). Peed out in late-night bars, en route via Turin, flushed down the toilet and into the river, the tenacious molecule still in tact and scientifically measurable. Indeed, a scientist took a mere beaker of water from the river and measured it. There was enough of the still-active drug in the liquid to cause a mild high in a laboratory chimpanzee.

Lack of Trust, forgetfulness, anger, volatility, low sperm count, aggravation, hostility, self-hatred, violence, low to no integrity, loss of personal accountability, spinning thoughts, obsessive tendencies, lack of reliability, lying, cheating, lack of personal hygiene are all possible odd behaviours the regular user exhibits. At its most extreme, getting into violent bloodshed or even killing others to get are possible. Zero personal responsibility. All these are common personal attributes of the Coke head. And these are becoming the very behavioural foundations our society is built on, with the drug's wide-spanning popularity. This, all this, is now acceptable among the minions.

If art mirrors life, let's take a look at the picture painted by Hollywood, for example. Look at what is being mirrored on and off screen. Our young people are growing up with that very portrait, an image of what's optional for them. And now, new, improved Coke use, with no judgments attached.

'Oh, he's just going through a stage.'

So permissive? So easily let go?

On either side of the border, tricks need to be turned to produce it, tricks to protect it. And then it turns tricks of the minds in the people receiving it on the other side.

* * * * * * * *

Maya had done her final Psych 451 paper in college on Crack Cocaine. Her prof had been very liberal with format and had encouraged articulate stylistic writing, with an almost journalistic edge. He wanted to prove that a 'compelling essay' was not an oxymoron. Maya was in writer's bliss that year.

Crack doesn't even look that ugly or surprising when one knows its vast appeal. It is so very accepted; it has no shock value any more.

Maya was surprised at the sadness she felt upon finding Theo, her ex-boyfriend from high school, living in a tent on the ugliest streets of east L.A., his life ruined from Crack in only 5 short years. Theo was the child of a well-known California endodontist and had been loved by his family from the get-go.

She was saddened when her best friend from high school, Lou-Lou, missed getting a decent job teaching after she was found positive in a random drug test before the school year commenced. She was saddened to learn that this had gone on Lou-Lou's professional record. That made it difficult for her friend to find work in the profession at all in the US in future. Might as well hand in the teaching certification, as if one had not spent well over $50 000 attaining it and countless nights up late studying for it.

Maya was more than sad, disappointed when her server at her favourite martini bar, where she took Zach for one of their first dates came to their table, evidently too high on coke or speed. She proceeded to flirt outrageously with Zach and then get the order wrong. Maya was sad that they didn't hire with more discernment, seeing as their cocktails started at $9.50 apiece. Had it caused a loosening of reality, forgetting reality entirely to an extent?

She was also more annoyed in a general sense that it appeared as thought those on Coke or coming off from the night before didn't have the integrity to see their own foolishness that so often reared up embarrassingly in public. It was like they thought themselves arrogantly 'above' the rest of non-wigged humanity, oblivious to their own saucer pupils, mood swings and inappropriate demands.

Maya was duly sad about that, as it just seemed so many were walking that road, as if the majority populous was so strung out it made it acceptable for all. She was saddened by the common apparent lack of standards. Did anyone say 'no' anymore?

Even ads on television seemed to target cracked out people, dumbing down the content, skewing the delivery mildly. Was it intentional? Who could say, but it was very weird for those people who chose not to go to the church of coke. It was as though the world was becoming more and more out to lunch, idiotic and permanently stupefied in a mire of drug-addled confusion.

'The world at large now geared for failures only. Successes a minority.'

Maya was in a minority of folks who valued maybe a glass of wine or two at the end of a long day, or even a puff of '*mota*' once in awhile. It wasn't a daily gotta-get-high thing nor was it in excess. This heavy white powder stuff was for fools. The people she respected and cared for had better things to do with their time. They didn't need it.

She was further saddened that she only had 5 friends and her own blood family to hang out with these days. Everyone else she knew was roofed out. Is it any fun to be around that when you're not interested or you fear the serious longer term damage that is inevitable? How about if a person has healthy self-esteem and thinks it looks just, well, sick?

Even the act of snorting powder looks dehumanizing. She imagined smoking a crack pipe didn't look too becoming either.

Maya was saddened that Anthony Kiedis, her favourite singer from The Red Hot Chili Peppers was on his way into hospital pre-Christmas 2008 after kidney failure, a likely result of years and years of drug use. She was sad that for him, it had appeared 100% out of control at times.

Maya was sad that for every 30 kids she had taught, there had been at least 6 in each class who had survived pregnancies and early childhood with drug-addicted parents. Maya was sad for the parents who carried unbearable burdens of guilt, as well as the kids who's ADD and/or imminent learning challenges were through the roof, likely linked in causative factors to you guessed it. Maya was sad for those kids, who may well not get opportunities others have due to their cognitive brain damage from drugs used before, during and after birth. Maya was sad that so many thought it was only the mother's pre and antenatal behaviours that affected a child's growth pattern, when, in fact, both sperm and egg, both mother and father imprinted the child permanently, through no choice of the youngster.

Maya was sad for the cute and seemingly brainy man she had met at a party once. He seemed so inspiring and easy to talk to. He seemed to think she was the best thing since sliced bread, her own ego bouncing along gaily as he held her captivated.

It wasn't until she realized he had to keep going to the bathroom to do yet another line to make him so inspired to engage that the depth of her sadness really hit her. He was so attractive and yet, with this realization, he appeared to dwindle into a small, shriveled, old man in a ball and chain, right before her eyes.

A few years later, that was a very near picture of his fate: no home, no car, no contacts, no job. He was done for, a vertical tombstone in a blackened alley, screaming out for some loose change to change the very life hr had orchestrated for himself due to utter loss of sensibility.

Maya was sad for the families of the mercilessly deceased and the families of the killers every time she looked at a Guadalajara paper.

Sadder still was she for the regular occurrences of horror.

She was sad for the tricks turned by street children to keep filling their pipes; children with no hope of reaching full adult-hood.

Maya went home and cried the day Octavio told her during Silent Reading Time in a quiet whisper at her desk that he had tried a bump at the beach with his 15-year-old cousin, Carlos, on their last family vacation.

It was everywhere.

And who wouldn't want to get high looking close up at this planet right now? We all need to get away from our 'stuff' sometimes. That's why partying is so hilarious. Everyone wants to get high. But at what cost?

Maya didn't realize that her sadness would come to rest at her feet through her very own classroom, with her ideals held high in a red, white and green banner of salvation flying above her head.

* * * * * * *

Chapter 8

Pensamientos

WEALTH & PROSPERITY "Gratitude" REAR LEFT Wood Blues, purples, & reds	FAME & REPUTATION "Integrity" REAR MIDDLE Fire Reds	LOVE & MARRIAGE "Receptivity" REAR RIGHT Earth Reds, Pinks, & whites
HEALTH & FAMILY "Strength" MIDDLE LEFT Wood Blues & Greens	CENTER · "Earth" · Yellow & earth tones	CREATIVITY & CHILDREN "Joy" MIDDLE RIGHT Metal White & Pastels
KNOWLEDGE & SELF-CULTIVATION "Stillness" FRONT LEFT Earth Black, blues, & greens	CAREER "Depth" FRONT MIDDLE Water Black & dark tones	HELPFUL PEOPLE & TRAVEL "Synchronicity" FRONT RIGHT Metal White, gray & black

"The unexamined life is not worth living"

Socrates

Octavio was getting tired of not seeing Juan. Increasingly, Juan needed to leave in the middle of the night. The boy missed his father, Sofia wisely noted. The maid had been privy to the innermost details of the Osegura-Vasquez family since before Octavio had arrived.

He had little interest in school. Certainly he could begin, but he could not finish his schoolwork. His teacher, Ms.Maya from California, told him that he had a wonderful imagination, but he had a hard time applying himself. It seemed Octavio's mind had no discipline and an increasing ability to wander as the year played on. In the US, he may certainly have been classified as ADD, but Maya was trying her best to teach non-coercively to bring out the riches of intellect in her lively students.

It was now late August, moving towards her extended holiday for Dia de Independencia, Sept. 16 - 18.

It commemorated the start of the Mexican Independence War by Father Miguel Hidalgo y Costilla, 1810. It would also commemorate the next time dear Maya was to see her beloved Zach. She was truly pining for him, longing for his touch and his familiar laughter by this point.

She loved the kids, though teaching them could be exhausting. Still, she found a ton of inspiration in her classroom. Maya was a born teacher. She could make any classroom work.

She loved their expression and lively spirits, their pride of nationality. Every night, she hit the pillow utterly spent from her days of giving to the max, answering their constant questions. Maya had never seen kids who loved their country the way these kids did, warts and all. Maya's previous American students were apathetic in relation really.

Maya was making yet another difficult discovery: this fierce national pride also held true in the staff room. As Maya's kind and effective teaching strategies revealed good results in her own brood of young learners, the rather militantly-trained Mexican teachers disliked her more and more. They didn't come right out and say it, but she became a victim of internal sabotage as they played subtle tricks to maker her days even more frustrating.

Odd looks in the hallways, incorrect reports of classroom conduct to the school Principal, outright mean language about her to her own students-each day became reminiscent of 9th Grade hallway treatment. Maya was being isolated and black-balled. She wasn't paranoid: it was brazen the closer they got to Dia de Independencia. All Maya felt like she had to look forward to was Zach's upcoming visit. She was not making friends of her colleagues clearly.

Maya took her lunch recess to write out her feelings in her trusty diary:

August 6/2009:

Why are they so Mean?

'Some of the Mexican women I teach alongside as colleagues are behaving like bitchy young girls. It is a very odd daily experience for me- unsettling and unnerving. I thought we all had our roles clearly defined here, and that I was just alongside them as an employee, another teacher in the classroom. It has never been quite this political-teaching-before. I mean there are the odd days back in the US for sure. I have wondered if Mrs. Olden, the quite possibly 76-year-old Science high school teacher was getting any as she has been quite shirty more than once. I later ate my words as I asked around about her and discovered her husband had died during our summer vacation. Then, I really felt like a bitch myself for even thinking such evil thoughts. I was 15 at the time.

But generally in any school I have worked at, though my experience is a mite limited still, there is a unified feeling of 'Let's Bond Here and Help One Another Out. This is Pretty Tough Work!'

Majority of the Mexican women staff at my day job are being little bitches. It is devolving into a kind of Them against Me. There is no way to get away from it any more; it's that in my face. Man, it's so hard being new to this country, not having the solid language skills I need yet, and dealing with this. I feel more alone than I ever have. They talk about me right in front of me, I know they do. The thing is, I can't decipher what they are saying yet! It just makes my blood boil. I feel sick when I'm near them.

They hate me and I don't have any idea why.

I wish I didn't have such a very thin skin. I suppose it allows me empathy in teaching, but it sure doesn't help in dealing with reality. Never has.

The bitches always do so much better than the sad little creatures that are all sensitive and weepy. Amongst women, survival of the fittest has never been so prevalent. I am reduced to Darwinian terms in my striving to further my career. Hopeless.

Damn it. I WILL learn their *lengua* and then I will know exactly what they are saying when they call me '*punta*' almost spitting it out as I walk in to get extra classroom materials or grab my lunch out of the staff room fridge. Last week, I asked another male teacher from Colorado to get my lunch out for me. I was just too intimidated.

I am such a scaredy cat. Why can't I just suck it up? It might even be in inverted or very backhanded *compliment*.

I am re-learning both personal boundaries and how to throw my own special brand o' full-on sass right back at little bitches in general now. I am so mad! My lunch break, a time that should be for quiet reflection and regeneration of energy for the afternoon's work, or even enjoyment of *comidas* is now spent ruminating on what the hell is going on. Why didn't I hang with more girls growing up? I might have learned better bitch tactics! I always played with the boys. They were so much fun and it was never weird. Ok, well, when I sprouted boobs, it did get a little weird. But never mean and spiteful and *excruciating* like this!

Later that day:

One thing I know is that I'm a kind gal. If another gal is being a little bitch, it is her issue. I don't even think like that. I feel fine about me; I don't get envious or competitive easily. It's not my way. I am not down with being a little bitch to other gals, so I try my damndest to be decent, even if it is a real strain some days. We all know Some Girls are just a pain in the royal ass, but so are some humans in general. I hope that people will grow through their foolishness. I am optimistic as I know I have had my own difficult times. The rough patches in life can make any of us behave like shit.

But these gals: it seems that true bitchiness is virtually *ingrained* in them, inseparable from their very souls. What must they think as they go to sleep at night? Are they on drugs to make them so mean? Why?

I just am so offended. I cannot fathom this kind of thing at all. Why do they waste their time trying so hard to be so cruel? It's like they *plan* it.

Fuckers. It's like they are mean to the deepest core, with absolutely no conscience about their actions at all. Am I expecting too much of humanity? I think maybe I am. How depressing.

My girlfriends in Cali are so cool! We love each other and always have fun. Support, caring tenderness, loyalty, ideas, love of music and foods together, the quintessential Friday vodka cocktail, cool sharing of clothes. I mean, My Girls, we bring each other Up! We are here for each other. I sure miss those gals *tons* right now.

Oh, I feel a tear. Fuck, I need to not cry. I have 13 more minutes before I have to teach again and Octavio will surely be making crazy noises as I go through Math, or sending paper airplanes to the lovely Damaris all class. I need my strength.

We're all women and it ain't an easy walk sometimes. I *get* that.

But, I need a backbone and NOW.

What I am learning:

She's likely a big one, if she is aiming that bad mojo in my direction, seeing as I only wanted to reach out in Love in the first place. A big irrational problem child: This Bitch.

I will no longer have my life joy, or my important work on this planet sabotaged by little bitches. That has come up for me too many times. Thoughtless, mean little bitches. Enough already.

And Jeez, there are just so *many*!

It's vulgar. Low-brow. Rude.

Why get on board?

Seems to be that being a genuine bitch, out to *really* needle someone else is a quick, impetuous response, a sad lack of personal evolution. Seeing as we already know how I feel about The Unevolved, and likely you feel the same way, I just cannot dignify a Little Bitch.

People who are not evolving every day are halting progress. And how I despise slowed progress. It doesn't mesh with my inner scientist. It insults my soul.

Right away, I become A Snob. Now, I will not be dealing with that individual for any longer than I have to. Being a bitch to others is yet another form of continuing Drama. Oh, The Drama!

Cut the drama, have a happy life.

Drama is close cousins with attention-seeking. Another abhorrence.

Save the drama for yo' mama (this slogan one of my adult night-school students came up with the other day. Oh, Josue! Thank you for reminding me of goodness!)

Now, I am very clear on why others become so deeply self-absorbed, another passive-aggressive form of being a little bitch: Retaliation. A way to 'even the score'. Oh, is that lack of evolution rearing its ugly head again? I see.

It comes to this then. It all boils down to the same shit.

It's about saving oneself, life preservation. Even if it is a very ill-thought out, low-brow way to be defensive.

I can do better than this. Frankly, I *can* and I *will*. Anger will be my motivator.

I can dance, laugh, sing, be free of negativity. I have friends, real friends. I have lifelong friends, whom I cherish.

Many are women. <u>None</u> are bitches.

We all have our unique creative gifts. I say: put time into what you CAN do and stay away from those who take from it. Yes, red flags are there to be acknowledged, even if it is a silent note to self. My tolerance for bitchy stupidity expired for the 100th time yesterday after a 57-hour work week began to wind down to lead me to today: Friday.

If you cannot shine and be 100% real with another, that person is not really *for* you at all, in truth. They are for them self.

<u>Know your way out</u>.

I am on a serious mission to detach any remaining bitch claws from my life.

(I write the next steps in red so I won't lose sight of what is needed here)

A rant of this magnitude wouldn't be complete without the offering up of a solution: next time I encounter a real bitch, I shall:

WHAT TO DO:

A.) Identify Bitch Issue Person. Look for Escape Route without delay. How can I rid my life of this destructive energy, this bitch? Know the way out. (Say to yourself: 'That shit don't fly with me! I'm too good to put up with this nonsense that isn't even *about me* in the first place')

NOTE:-it's never really about you. It's their story.

B.) Breathe deep into your belly and count to 10, remembering that a Goddess does not resort to the same idiot way of being. A Goddess is a Goddess and out to captivate the universe. A bitch is out to sabotage anyone is her midst. The two are opposite.

C.) Make the choice: I am a Goddess, I will, thus, SHINE. Grab your integrity, load up your duffel bag of Hope and Glory to hop onto The Highroad. Run for it...

D.) Hold dignity close to your heart, load GRACE into your gun holster.

E.) Fuck compassion. That's sooo 90's. She's being *a bitch*. There's no excuse. Who cares how she feels, she's a danger and, thus, a very real problem. You only get what you give.

F.) And off we go! Bu-bye. Go find a Goddess or an animal or a fine man to rock on with instead. Enjoy a flower. Sit for a graceful moment. Watch the ocean: strong yet peaceful.

G.) Let It Go. Move on and *fast*.

OK, it's time to teach Math here. No more griping.'

* * * * * * * *

Octavio had perfected the art of paper airplanes. He designed jets, the kind that his Daddy flew in, and he sent them out over the playing field when it was recess; he sent them to Damaris' beautiful head during class also. Octavio never grew tired of staring out the window during Math class. He was not held in any way by school.

Strangely though, Ms. Maya was getting through to him. He loved doing research projects and missed almost no details when it came to finding out about gorillas or what Germany can be thanked for in terms of international imports. Octavio was learning he was especially good at understanding how things worked. Ms. Maya often encouraged him to design machines. He loved her for seeing this. She understood!

Octavio needed a solid place, as he never felt too solid at home. Sure, he was loved and fed well. He knew he was wanted. He did not, however, see how his brain was of use. No one outside of school took a lot of interest in it. Daddy told him that he would have all the riches in the world whether he listened in class or not. Mama was a little stricter with her son, but still indulged him at every opportunity. Octavio knew a lot about manipulation, he knew a lot about video games, but he didn't have a real understanding of how to treat other people.

Maya was perceptive, a natural facilitator of her students. She sensed this about Octavio in how she planned each lesson so she had back-up plan for redirection if need be. This allowed him to flourish as he'd not done before and minimized classroom interruption to her other students. In a successful classroom, a teacher has to think equally about the shape of each child's ego as she does about the topics to be covered. Today, Octavio would play doctor, as they were learning about human anatomy and the knee reflex was to be covered in class. He did love to be on stage-this, the perfect role.

'Octavio, please come up to the front of the classroom. I will need you to call your 'patients' names out, one by one. Then, each child can hop up here on my desk, and you will use your medical mallet to hit their just under their knee caps, one by one. This should result in an involuntary knee-jerk reaction. This way we can see what involuntary reactions are in the nervous system.'

Octavio was happy to oblige. Finally, he got to be Someone Somewhere. He did just this, but after 6 students had tried, he lost interest and asked if someone else could play doctor instead. He felt his brain slipping out the window. He wasn't really at school anymore, but had entered a world of special effects, blasts, dings and whistles instead. Octavio had duly entered the call of Super Mario Brothers.

This issue had been recurring with him slipping off to his Never-Never Land. Maya made a note to herself to try to engage with young Octavio in this regard after class. The lesson went on without Octavio's full mental presence. She could only do so much.

The recess bell rang, signaling playground duty.

* * * * * * * *

Maya was talking with other staff on the playground. She stuck to the ones that would not shoot her evil glares or try to tell her *'no moleste'* (don't interfere) in a tone heavy with condescension if she even so much as spoke to a child who was in their classes. When sufficient questions were asked amongst the other international teachers, it began to come clear to her: money was coming into and out of the school that was unrelated to the school itself. This was weird. She could see parents donating on behalf of their own kids, but why would money be leaving the school coffers? They kept hearing in staff meetings that they needed to save costs, to raise more money for the school, and yet there was no published fiscal record as there generally was in other private schools. Maya had suggested a school garage sale and had helped to organize it. They had not seen a centavo of the income it generated and had no clear idea where the money was going.

The Swine Flu was reported seemingly all of a sudden at about the same time as Maya toyed with these questions about her chosen place to teach. It was everywhere, spreading from Mexico City north and into the US, the media said. They thought they may even have to break from school early this year to allow for 'Swine Flu quarantine'. It was bizarre. Maya had never seen an outbreak of flu hit so hard, so fast. Why was it not reported in other areas of the country like Oaxaca, where there was considerably higher rates of poverty and filth? It seemed to be primarily a Mexico City/Guadalajara thing. It was reported all over the world to be spreading rapidly. Hitting younger people, the reports said. The school announced it would keep tight measures on what was transpiring health wise in order to protect both staff and students. If need be, they would insist on taking 10 days taken off from school, a preventative measure for 'Swine Flu H1N1', as the 'pandemic' might soon spread the globe, a sweep of fear in its wake.

These topics were passed around the playground with strong cautions, of 'get enough sleep', 'watch those raw fruits and veggies', 'be careful with your health' to all the foreign teachers. The US didn't host the same level of unchecked amoebic parasites that Mexico did. Mexico seemed like a veritable Petri dish, making new enemies of humans all the time. And yet these Mexican people laughed harder than anyone back home, made more light of life, accepted death better, with much less resistance to it. They knew how to party for the brevity of life abounded so it was all 'live for today'. It might be difficult for a foreign teacher to with stand the kinds of illness that were evident, let alone to really delve into the culture. Maya found it all interesting, but was feeling less and less inclined to make her life here after being in it for over 7 weeks. She was appreciative of the many conveniences home in California offered now she had been away for awhile.

Maya had come to this land to learn. She hadn't brought much, but her college education allowed her a lot in Mexico. She had her additional night job teaching business negotiations English at the nearby Honda car factory, Japanese owned and operated, in Salto, about one hour outside Centro. The young woman had more work than she knew what to do with. She was working a lot, but she was making a considerably good income with all the hours, capping out at the equivalent of about $1300 US per month. An average accountant in Mexico made about $1500 US or $15000 pesos per month; this was looked at as a very handsome income. Maya was considered a yuppie buy Mexican standards.

She missed her man and her life back home regularly. She questioned why she came all too often. Maya made good on her time there, swinging from job to job every day on her bike, distracting herself from feelings of isolation and missing Zach. She missed him and just having the company every day. She had in her mind that she would fulfill this contracted teaching year, likely to return to her native land. She knew Zach had a visit planned in the next few weeks. It was all bearable, if tiring.

Maya brought an open mind, a keen sense as a teacher on many levels and so she was utilized in as many ways as Mexico could find to have her. This year was serving a career-enhancing, language-acquiring purpose.

The bell rang for end of lunch hour recess. It was time to get the kids in a group and bring them in. Maya stood up a little higher on the steps and smiled at her students. They loved her. It didn't take much to get them ready to open the books and initiate experiments for science.

As the children lined up, giggling at some recess joke, Maya was distracted by Ms. Josie, coming her way. Ms.Josie was the school registrar and receptionist.

'Maya, we would like to meet with you to discuss some good news,' she came to the teacher to tell her.

Maya was curious. She wished she could know a little more, but the kids needed to get moving and it wasn't appropriate to ask.

'Sure. What time can we meet?'

'How about 4 pm today, after classes?' Ms. Josie responded with a gentle smile

'Ok, good. I'll be there.' Maya answered, turning back to the kids and motioning them inside.

The day moved along fairly effortlessly. Maya was good at planning. Her ideas were original; her students loved her. She would wake at 5 am, with the rooster crowing on the neighbour's rooftop and the church bells ringing at Templo San Bernardo, on Plan de San Luis, down the way from her apartment. This was an exercise to get clear on the day every day, seeing as her day's commitments were easily 12 - 15 hours long regularly. Maya had her lessons keyed up and prepped in her mind well before class. If she failed to prep even one part of any of her lessons, she'd drop the ball; a fate that she felt was only for loser teachers and unfair to fee-paying students' families.

Ethics don't fly well in the face of corruption. Just as mediocrity can't stand excellence, ethics and the people who have them are thwarted when majority have none.

In the back of her head was this curiousity about the meeting, as well as the knowledge that there might be something up. She had never felt this way at school before, so she really wasn't sure what to make of it. Maya had been accused of being highly sensitive in her life. Sometimes, she was borderline psychic. Other times, she put it down to hormones or being tired as she might tend to see things that may not have been so real in an elevated sense. She knew all this and yet the prevailing thoughts were not quite right, a little off somehow.   Lessons were taught, bells rang. Finally, the day was wrapping up.

Maya went to Octavio as he packed his backpack up for the day and asked him if she could speak to him quietly. He looked at her, nodded. She bent down so that she could look him in the eyes.

'Octavio, for some time now, it feels like you're not really 'there' with us in class. It feels as your teacher, like your mind is somewhere else. What do you think about this?' Maya asked, firmly but kindly.

Octavio hesitated.

'I don't know teacher. I never see my Daddy. I miss him. Sometimes, I don't feel like being at school, but more I feel I want to be with my dad.' Octavio said clearly, in English with a heavy Mexican accent.

Maya got that. His dad had been at school only a handful of times, but when he was there, he certainly engaged with a few different people. It seemed like Octavio's dad, Juan, was never there without the Principal, Sergio. Maybe he was a benefactor of the school of some kind. Some people did these things quietly. Octavio needed something to help his flailing grades, that was for sure.

'Octavio, you need to ask your dad to do stuff with you then. You need to tell him that this is how it feels for you.' Maya said. This needed to be treated very carefully. Tuition was being paid, there were expectations from the families on a lot of these kids, and only more so, on a foreign teacher.

Octavio looked down. He felt a tear trying at his eye, but he didn't want Ms.Maya to see tears. He tried to be a big boy.   He felt like he spent half his life trying to get more time with his father. He felt like he had tried and his dad wasn't going to give him any more than he did already. Octavio would see more gifts than he would real time with Juan. He knew it deep down.

'When you come here to school, I need you to be here with us. It's not hard work all day. I try to make the lessons interesting for you guys. We have fun as well as learn in my class. Come on, work with me, Octavio.' Maya said.

'OK, Teacher. I'll try.' Octavio looked up at her then down again, a little ashamed and scared his mother would arrive to see him talking to his teacher. 'Will you tell my mom?' he looked right at Maya, expecting an answer.

'No, Octavio. If you can give me a little more focus and try closing the circle once you open it, I think we can move forward without getting your mom or dad involved. Can we make that our plan?' Maya asked with genuine respect for the little man who was obviously feeling a lot about this matter.

'Yes, we can. I will try better for you, Ms.Maya,' Octavio looked at her with a crooked smile.

He liked his teacher, he knew she was kind. He knew she would do her best with him. He would try to live up to what she was requesting. At least he didn't ever have to go back to the mean old boring Ms.Lala, who'd been his teacher last year. She had hated him and made that very clear to the young boy. It only made his grades fall lower to have his teacher sink along with him. Ms. Maya was different. Octavio was glad of that. At least she tried to understand where he was at. That made Octavio want to try.

He walked out; down the hall he went his little shoulders relieved a smidge somewhat of the burden of missing someone beloved.

* * * * * * *

Chapter 9

Promocion

'Failure is the condiment that gives success its flavor.'

Truman Capote

Maya needed to pick up some more books and then to go to her after school meeting. She gathered her belongings and headed out to the Principal's office. Ms.Josie and Sergio were there waiting for her. They had a chair pulled up for her and everyone had a glass of purified ice water with lime and mint. This was clearly planned to the last letter.

Sergio was fairly direct in his approach, but cordial. He only ever spoke top Maya with respect, but was not often at the school. Maya always felt there were questions she would like to ask, but saw little opportunity.

'Maya, we invited you here today, as we will need to make some changes in staff for the next school year. Already, we can see your good efforts and we are thinking well ahead to secure the best people.'

'OK, so what does that mean for me?' she asked. She had been mildly distracted by Sergio's eyebrows, which fanned wildly over his eyes like black raven wings.

'Maya, in fact,' he said clearly and with a thick accent, 'we want to look at having you on board as our Principal next year. I have other things I need to attend to and cannot be that person next year.' Sergio replied. He seemed a bit stern in his approach to her, but at times, the language was worked through with different inflections when it was a second language. And Maya was feeling a little sensitive after the day was ending so she paid little heed to her insides.

Ironically, at that very moment, Maya needed to trust her gut more than she ever had.

'Whoa. I totally wasn't expecting that,' Maya replied, slightly awed and flattered. 'Can I think about this?' she asked, hesitant to make any solid moves right away. It was only the very end of August. She hadn't been teaching for this school for very long to make such a big step. In the US, you had to put in at least 10 or 15 solid years of teaching and even attain a Masters before being considered for Principal.

She was blown away. She wondered if the same staff would be there next year.

'Yes, of course. So then we need to hear back from you if you're not interested as soon as possible, of course,' Sergio said, a little surprised that someone would even need time to think about a promotion. He remained hopeful but appeared calm, in fact, quite smooth, in front of Ms.Josie and Maya. Sergio: the master of appearances.

He was certain she'd say yes. The business was wrapped up in his mind. The Others would be so pleased. His thoughts shifted comfortably to how he'd entertain his lover that night with caviar, French champagne and a good romp to Michael Jackson's, 'Off the Wall', their very favourite. Anything could be got in Mexico on the black market.

There was a fair bit in it for her, of course, a young woman with a career in front of her. She was a damned good teacher. He had chosen her for her grace. She was disarming and effective at her job. She was obedient as a staff member, never asking too many questions or taking up too much of his time.

Maya would be the perfect figure heard for the school. Being able to advertise an international school was a hot seller to the private school community in Guadalajara. They loved teachers from the US, Canada, South Africa, England, New Zealand, Australia. It was not so easy to get good certified help, considering the fiscal translation of the Mexican peso worldwide. Maya represented everything they needed at the time and she came in a pretty, professional little package. Maya as their principal and cover: a value-added American product in a place that revered North America and valued learning English. This would certainly put a luster finish on the underpinnings of the school. The free world could be accessed by those who knew how to speak both Spanish and English. Maya embodied what they needed.

They'd already discovered she worked like a mule and didn't complain about it. How much more could they reap from the naïve girl? They looked forward to what they could juice from the *Gringa* in the future. She was practically theirs. She represented all they hated in terms of Mexican-American history, and so they did not feel badly about putting her at risk, either on the playground or nationally. They delighted equally in the idea that she would deliver a high return for them, just by staying on.

There was no love in this promotion.

Maya, still a bit stunned, thanked Ms.Josie and Sergio and she was out the door. Her head always needed about an hour after classes to get clear again before she went on to teach in the evening. This was news she hadn't anticipated. It was a lot to think about. She first wondered, 'Why? Why would they choose me?'

She just kind of wanted to return home to her boyfriend. That was coming up a lot, the feeling of not being sure about staying long-term, or just being there at all. She missed the surf and sun in California and was in an inland city of 6 million here in Guadalajara. She felt landlocked after years of living not far from the ocean. She realized she missed lots of things: books in English in engrossing bookstores, music and culture she loved and knew well, her friends, her family, good wine, cheese and chocolate, safe sex. These things came bounding forward in her mind. She failed to salivate over the 'opportunity' in front of her, failed to let her vocational success carry her on this one. There was something odd about this rushed flattery.

Guadalajara was cool; it had lots to offer, certainly for 12 or 13 months. But could she stand the heat, the pollution, traffic, constant noise, the blunt sexism, the buzzing craziness of it for her whole life? What about Zach? Could she really convince him to move his own life down here with her? Would that mean that she would then become a Mexican in the end, selling out on her true roots?

What about the Mexican staff? They would HATE her now. She must keep this very secret. Now, they might be really jealous and even fiercer to her. Her origins meant a great deal to her, the reverence of bloodline a vital part of most Jewish families. She could not miss the Passover Seder two years in a row. Her mother would be too disappointed. It was all a lot to think about.

Maya wasn't sure she wanted to stay once the option was there in front of her, higher pay and all. Her mind went to the possibilities of teaching nearer the ocean, maybe relocating; Zach would warm to that easier, she felt. He'd salsa dance with her because she loved it, not because it was his natural talent. She would have to fashion a for them both, life where he could surf and enjoy his own things, too.

She slung her pack over her left shoulder, unlocked her bike after grabbing a strong coffee on the way, deep in thought, and she was off to figure it out. Off to make her commute through the streets of Guadalajara to her middle class Colonia (neighbourhood), Mezquitan Country, where she rented her apartment, near Plan de San Luis, off Enrique Diaz de Leon. She had two hours before her next adult class in Business Negotiations English. They were advanced students, full of valid questions, and she really had to focus with them. It was serious business.

Maya needed to weigh out some details.

As she whizzed towards her front gate, she looked up in the late afternoon Mexican sun. A flashing green hummingbird sped by overhead. She took a deep breath. The scent of jasmine engulfed her for a moment.

* * * * * *

Chapter 10

Captivo

'Those not for you are against you'

-Bob Dylan, circa 1969

Bettos had kept his eye on Gustavo's movements via Centro for a few months. He had spotted the small boy with his exceptional agility and had decided this street child would be a perfect candidate for a new life.

He moved with care and precision, always calm, a kind demeanor. Bettos was well-versed in the art of convincing others. They already had a regular mule. They need what Gustavo what could do for them. They were due to make another run to Colima and then fly the next kilo of pure uncut out of Puerto Vallarta. They needed two mules for every kilo. Bettos needed a mule.

There was no time to wait. It had to happen within the next 10 weeks, with careful training, explanation and orchestration of every detail of the run. Their leg of the cartel had only seen an increase in volume being successfully shipped thanks to new US/Mexico border controls and their regular recipient on the other side. They needed the new mule and more product; neither could wait.

It was flying faster than ever into the US and Canada, up the west coast. On the east side of the country, it made its way into Europe, pumping the party kids in Paris up, rocking Ibiza and creating the worst of needs all over Italy. Mexico was the elbow of white speedy powder movement in the world to date. The land of transcendence and poignant bloody history, the Mexican pride, had become the revered connection of trafficking production up from Columbia, El Salvador, Nicaragua, Panama, and Columbia. Mexico was losing its identity to drug movement. Costa Rica was reported to be producing big, too, but was keeping their production local, likely due to the poor economy still struggling with risk. In time, Mexico would convince the little player that it had some grand designs in store and Costa Rica would also sell out.

Bettos and Juan were responsible for moving the stuff and gaining more market power and access. The sweet talkers of the trade and some of the highest risk players in the black market.   Hence, they traveled frequently out of their heads on drugs in order to sustain the energy required to fuel such high adrenaline activities.

They made one run and they had to turn around almost immediately to plan the next or they'd lose the customer. They could not lose the customer. Bettos was aware that Juan was working with supply lines and suppliers. Bettos had his own share in the product flow line up and he knew what needed to be done.

He sharpened up his schpiel about what riches lay in the Promised Land and headed to Centro to try to find Gustavo. They had covered all the bases but they needed the mule. The more easily disposable, the better. Yet, they couldn't take just anyone. There were defined character traits to seek out to secure the mule. Bettos knew from stalking the street child that Gustavo had what it takes.

* * * * * * *

Gustavo had settled into a corner of an ancient library that still ran for the public, albeit slowly. The librarian was an 88-year-old widower and though she was enthusiastic about literature, she claimed that all others apart from her dead husband could wait their turn. She was in no hurry for anyone and her shuffling gait illustrating this without her need for words. It was common knowledge in the vicinity of the city. You wanted free books to borrow, to learn from? You waited.

Gustavo figured as much in a mere 10 seconds of studying her. He found his own way.

Gustavo had come in about mid day, looking for a newspaper, or anything she had that she could loan him to read. She'd found him a current paper as well as a book on '*dinosarios*' that really interested the young boy. He spent the remainder of the afternoon, huddled over the Sports section, trying to attain the words he could use to describe plays and his growing adoration and understanding of Mexican sports heroes. It was his dream to go to a real live soccer game at Stadio Jalisco one day.

The librarian busied herself in the dusty corridors, pushing books back a little, dusting them off, picking them up to have a look at a page or two. The two were thoroughly comfortable. Not one other person entered the library to take out a book that afternoon.

Eventually, Gustavo felt his stomach burn and knew he must try to find Ana Lisa and food or both before sundown. He thanked the librarian. He would be back as soon as he could, his thirst for knowledge growing daily.

'Vaya con Dios! (Go with God!)' She called out after him as he scuttled off.

'Gracias, Ustedes!' Gustavo called back to her.

A friend with access to books was just what he needed. He would go to her to see if she had a book on *'tiburones'* (sharks) next. Some day, he would get down the coast of Mexico, past the cliff jumpers in Acapulco. He would get to Puerto Escondido and beyond into the fierce tides of Ziplolite and swim in waters that sharks inhabited. He imagined he would learn how to surf and coast right over their jagged fins. He was not afraid but fascinated. Learning was changing his world. He was like a porifera, absorbing knowledge at stealth speed. He couldn't get enough of all the words. It was as if he sat deciphering a code and every new syllable brought him a step closer to literacy. The world was his as it had never been before. He thought he might be feeling something called *'successo.'*

Gustavo ran on, past the front patio area of Coyote Rojo, on into the area beyond McDonald's on Juarez. He smelled and ran, smelled and ran, wishing with every pore of his being that he could eat something somewhere. He ran until he had nothing to run with. He ran until he felt himself sink into a place of eerie blinding light and growing quiet. His eyes saw only what was in front of him; his brain began to do tricks. He knew it: his blood sugar was plummeting again; he was close to a faint. He could not see properly.

Gustavo knew this same feeling on almost a daily basis.

Just as he could hardly stumble on, a familiar hand came out to block his fall and his movements forward. Bettos was there, just as he needed to be at the critical second.

'Careful, Little One. Running crazy like this. You are hungry again; I can see it in you.' Bettos said patiently to Gustavo. Let me get you something.'

By this point, Gustavo had no pluck left in him. He could not muster his fight, though he some bizarre, unexplained danger surrounding Bettos. Did this anomalous yet familiar man breed content in him or contempt? Gustavo didn't yet have the wisdom of experience to know, only his street smarts. He needed food and water badly, as he did by the end of most of his days. He had not grown much since last year.

Bettos got Gustavo over to a safer spot. He fanned the boy's face to try to help stop the faint from overcoming the child. He then went for food. He returned with two *gringos* (a cheese and bean or meat filled larger size soft taco), one for each of them, and a cool *horchata* (the sweetened rice milk popular in the area) for the young Gustavo.

He had to hold Gustavo upright for the boy to ingest some nourishment. Gustavo was still dizzy, but the sweet cold horchata took him to a new place quickly. He was so grateful. Peace fell upon him, he calmed himself. He was stunned, satiated and thankful as anyone could be after 5 solid minutes of eating and drinking, with no other means of providing it for themselves. His eyes revealed his vulnerability yet he didn't try to put a front on for the stranger. He still knew the danger in Bettos but beggars could not be choosers. Bettos watched as Gustavo took the food by storm, literally cramming as much of it into his *pequeño* mouth at one time as he could.

He was satisfied. An extraordinary event.

Gustavo sprang back to life with the resilience of youth. He had tossed caution to the wind this once, as his body flooded with gratitude for Bettos. What a fine day it had been! First the quiet librarian, who found him reading material and then left him to his own devices to devour it. Then, seeing Bettos again, good Bettos who was feeding him and had been kind with food in the past.

In a desperate place, kindness takes on a different shade of justice. Even the most miniscule kindness offered can lift a heavy burden of frustration. This is what transpired between the two that afternoon.

Bettos had been born into a family of five children. His father had not stayed beyond his conception and had left a destitute and ill-equipped mother to raise the children alone.

Bettos had watched his otherwise quiet, fragile, petite mother duke it out in the streets for her children each day. Bettos knew the sting of living in shame. He had never felt respect as a human life in the true sense of the word. He had seen his mother grovel and beg, in order that her children, not even she could be fed. This had etched upon his mind at a tender age the death sentence of survival in Mexico. He had seen it all, the dogs running the streets with massive dripping tumours out their backsides, the filth in gutters, the pornographic back alley hook-ups between businessmen and prostitutes, the gay men hoofing drugs off one another's' chests outside bars. Bettos had seen the ugliest humanity had. He wanted a new day for his life. Otherwise, he saw no reason to continue on.

Getting out of Mexico to start afresh in the US or anywhere else was never easy for a born Mexican. Opportunity did not avail itself easily to the average Mexican. Bettos was a Mexican-born man trying to make a better life than poverty. And, so he went about designing the most clever and unsuspecting cartel he could conjure. He found his guy friends from the old days and they, too, wanted a New Day, some kind of Hope. The country they were born into was not behind them, it was in no shape to be. Their Mexico was on her own last legs. They would have to fend for themselves if they wished to stay proudly Mexican.

They put together everything they had, plus some they borrowed and they set up a coke circuit. Each player had their own defined, discussed Area of Responsibility within the mafia. There was no debate about carrying guns. You wanted in, you needed a gun. You never knew. The whole deal held a high degree of responsibility. A lot of the urchins he'd known in his youth just weren't up to the task, too wasted on years of drugs or self-deprecating activities had ruined their immune systems. Majority were too embroiled in the petty dramas of each day, heavy laden with their machismo bravado. The type to pull it off was somehow smarter, more refined. It took a Quality X that was uncommon, and a willingness to keep one's wits sharp.

They worked secretly, frequently by night. It all started in Bettos' roomy apartment, downtown, on Priscilano Sanchez, not far from where Elisa had worked at Estacion de Lulio.

Bettos and Juan were the main guys in that ring, back in 1999. Sergio had a stake, as did Elisa through Juan. Octavio was merely a beneficiary when they all realized their friends would be having children who needed an education. This was faultless. They would have a good-looking, intelligencia geared school to clean up the cartel money and bring in more, while the cartel itself could keep product moving under this guise. More ironic was how busy the Mexican policia were, trying to deal with the bloodbath that the compilation of Mexican cartels was causing every hour of every day in the country. The cops were either busy or, in some cases, involved underground in taking the drugs off one cartel and then selling them again through another, maybe doing some as the progression went. It was utter mayhem to the Western eye. A labyrinth of secrets, lies and corruption laced the entire black-market industry. Likely, Bettos, Juan and their cohorts would not be easy suspects if they played the game they way they knew they should, the way they knew Mexico went and had done for eons.

It was a set up. The cartel had been in existence, producing and moving the best of the best for ten years. Each year had been a greater success, the kind that is so unexpected, it is difficult to hide. Each year, Elisa received more presents. Octavio was privy to a decent education in English no less, the *lengua* of *libertad*.

More and more year-long contracts went out to foreign and unwitting teachers who joined the crew. At the school, they came all the way from their homelands, with requisite certificates to educate the children of the elite of Guadalajara's doctors, politicians, teachers, accountants, store owners, lawyers in the city; right alongside the folks who earned their keep Narco trafficking. Many sacrificed 11 years or more of family vacations with both parents working full time to send their children to the school that was being used as a money laundering operation, completely unbeknownst to the very clients upholding its backbone.

Sergio made sure to attain a copy of Maya's California teaching certification upon her arrival at the school. This was a very valuable piece of paper in the circle indeed. This bright idealist would make a perfect Principal to add a placid sheen to their racquet. He would see to it that she was plied with a pay raise and a bonus career boost if she could play along, keeping her mouth shut. He assumed money would talk to her the way it did to the rest of them. Everyone became a pawn in the game in the view of the school/mafia, just the way everyone is a cartel is a player. The only difference is that generally those in a cartel know they're in it. This was, perhaps, that much more disturbing as Maya had no idea the risk she was being exposed to, nor did any of the well-intentioned teachers from overseas.

Once Gustavo had come back to reality, he saw that he must try to connect with Ana Lisa, pronto or she would go out into the dangerous night on an empty belly again. This was always scary for both of them.

Gustavo waited for her tiny footsteps every day at dawn. If she was late, or God forbid, didn't come at all or even for a good many hours, he panicked. He would become paralyzed waiting for her. Gustavo knew what time it was by looking at the sun's place on the sidewalk shadows. He felt so much better now that his hunger had gone, he almost felt giggly. Yet, this was serious. Ana Lisa was the one person he felt Love for in his unformed world.

'Bettos, I must go to Ana Lisa. She will be waiting for me and I want her to know what I have learned about *dinosarios* and soccer today, Señor'

'Of course, niño. I understand you need to see your friend. But you must first let me tell you about how you can have food and a good life every day. Now that you know me, you are fortunate. I have some ideas to help you with your plight.' Bettos said, referring to Gustavo's street life.

'OK, but I must go now. I can meet with you perhaps tomorrow or the next day?' Gustavo felt urgency, like Ana Lisa was calling to him. He was keen on getting away from there, still feeling weird around this Bettos feeding person, still a mystery.

'Well, the project I'm working on right now doesn't have that much time, Gustavo. I would need you soon, but could guarantee you three meals a day and a new life in about a week.' Bettos spoke softly but with an air of importance and respect for his daily dealings. He was an authority, knowing just the right method acting techniques to employ to instill genuine belief in this child.

'Bettos, if I miss Ana Lisa again, she will be cross with me. I swore to the Virgin de Guadalupe that I would meet her for dinner this evening. We were going to run across the town, trying for scraps. Even though I have been fed, she has not. I cannot leave her waiting for me, Bettos!' Gustavo tried to hurry off, but Bettos blocked him, this time more insistent.

'I can give you an *oro* (gold) ticket that would allow you to feed yourself and Ana Lisa every night, no more running. Trust me, Niño. The world I can show you is like nothing you have ever seen before.' Bettos tried the more captivating line of debate, still not allowing Gustavo physical passage.

Gustavo was frustrated by this impediment, but he admitted to himself he was also deeply curious.

'OK, Bettos. You win. What is this about?' Gustavo reasoned that he would disappoint Ana Lisa this once in order that he and she may be united in a more fiscally reverent way in the future. No one had ever offered him a way out of Centro before. Soon, he would be a man and would need a real source of income. Perhaps Bettos was onto something that could open some kind of doors for dear inquisitive Gustavo.

As Gustavo turned back, Bettos put his arm around the child and steered him towards the schoolyard. 'This way, you can have a life of learning, and food and shelter and a home. You have made the right choice. Let me show you where you can go to school now.'

School. What a concept. This meant learning every day. This meant projects about *tiburones* and Sports Days and festivals, music, friends. Gustavo was so taken in by these ideas of Bettos, each one a dream of his, that he let Ana Lisa slip away for the moment. He was being taken in. Gustavo could not stop the vortex he was circling. Enticed by knowledge that he would not have had otherwise, the child was game.

Bettos knew already he had scored his mule. Greasy, greedy glee spread through him like oil after an oceanic leak, uncontained.

* * * * * * *

Chapter 11

Detales

"We are only partially in control of our own creativity. It has its own agendas."

-verbal quote from an artist friend of Maya's over the Best Latte in Santa Monica, 2006

Maya had discovered the downtown library a few weeks back. A slice of cooling peaceful Heaven in otherwise constantly 'on' Guadalajara. It became another spot for refuge for Maya at the end of the working week, when she needed to plan and collect her thoughts. As well, it served to deepen her understanding of the language. It familiarized her further with the spectrum Mexican literary talent, always a treat. Carlos Fuentes was a recent discovery. She had decided she enjoyed both Mexican and Indian cinema and literature best, alongside Isabel Allende, the beloved Chilean author. Her mission for the end of the next calendar month was to embark on the book 'Paula' by Allende, a Chilean writer and political descendent, with plenty of passion of her own. Maya would read the whole book in Spanish. It helped she had read and cried while reading it in English already. The interpretation would be easier with a basal understanding of the events.

As Maya sat quietly, a stack of Mexican books in Spanish on her one side and her student's History tests from this week on the other, she sat and mused. Was there really any point to being such a passionate person? She was here in a place full of zeal, music and art and yet so many appeared blasé in the wake of intensity in their near midst. Scourging heat from the unrelenting sun, constant tensions and lack of predictability amongst the mass Narco Traficante and Policia's ongoing feuds-the nation still at a standstill in terms of justice. Domestic violence, poverty, crime, sickness-it all featured in each day's walk to or from school, through various colonias and levels of income.

All the while, in stark contradiction, the most stunning music played, writers and artist produced, children laughed, mothers sang to their babies, love was made, food enjoyed. The ardor was there, but a resignation had grown up equally strong in the Mexican peoples, apparent in both those of education and those with none. It was as if Maya detected a cultural resignation, a collective voice uttering, 'What can we do?'

There is no escaping an uninsured country. The idea of social class exists in Mexico, just as it does in most places of capital means. Born without, stay without. The 'haves' move on through. In the eyes of an educated, upper class Californian it seemed wayward, the idea that one could not create one's own manifest destiny. That was what the US was built on: immigrants with their own wares coming together since the dawn written history in a melting pot to make more.

Never enough to really instill fear in Maya; she was not that ignorant. Only to cue her to ask yet more questions. Her thoughts rang with ceaseless curiousity. She could study Mexico all she wanted, but she would always be California born, of Jewish blood, a neurosurgeon's child with a fussy, controlling mother. Our Maya was practically a classic case study of the end-product of a high-strung west coastal Jewish community in the best part of the state. Maya felt cookie cutter. She was a mere observer here, with a ticket out when she chose.

This baby was not born to suffer.

She could no sooner renounce her roots than she could paint her skin chocolate syrup brown. She adored the skin of Mexico. She could try to understand and have a heart, maintain compassion here, but how could she realistically empathize? She was a child of privilege in one of the most economically resilient countries in the world. She would never suffer the way she saw suffering here. There were always catchments for a little princess of this nature; it was a given.

Yet, she knew that her favourite taco stand on Juarez Ave downtown could go under any day. Or that her neighbour Rosa would not heal her arthritis due to lack of knowledge about serious nutrition and a very real lack of money.

* * * * * * * *

Her mind was wandering like a nomad, place to place, thing to thing. In time, Maya hoped she might travel to see Nepal to study Buddhism and to understand the culture better there. She hungered to know how others did it, what their traditions were; why they succeeded or failed as nations.   The ideas around Buddhism helped her cope; though she saw she was coping with so very little in comparison the more she looked, the more her eyes opened. Maya felt gratitude and sadness at the same time. She knew she was born into something that was hers. Eureka: she was beginning to unravel what the anger of her Mexican school colleagues may have been concerning.

Maya had been on a brief trip to India when she was 19, a cultural exchange her father thought pivotal to his daughter's gaining a complete understanding of the globe. (He felt she MUST go to Israel, India and China to see clearly what this world spins on) She had gone with her previous goy high school friend, Lorna, likely never to speak to her again afterwards.

India itself she found to be a challenge as a travel, though continuously fascinating. She was facing the incandescent beauty of the land at sunset, amidst the inevitable harrowing suffering in the streets. She'd not had nearly enough time there to see what she wanted and planned to stay on longer to explore a bit more. It was, after all, pennies a day to be there. Maya was making good on the equivalent of about $5 per day of spending money, including accommodations. She was getting good at outsmarting India and her dear Daddy encouraged her to stay longer, of course. It would take a lifetime to see India really.

Maya was loving her newfound sense of pure freedom and independence, writing the most vivid e-mails about it home daily. From the idli she snacked on at lunch to the breezy rooftops of Pushkar, she felt immense inspiration in the diverse land. Her father was enjoying the distraction of her verse over coffee each morning from imminent neurosurgery cases that would greet him by 9 am.

Maya and Lorna had veered off course together after the part of the trip that was with the group was over. Maya had designs on going it solo, but Lorna had said she *really* wanted them to do it together. Lorna convinced her on grounds of personal safety, at the very least, she'd said. Maya got sucked in, only to regret it later.

Perhaps it had to do with the foul taste left in Maya's mouth after the The Mumbai Incident. Not one she'd even told her trusted diary, it was so direly foul.

Sadly, Maya never got over it.

They had pulled up to a fairly decent hotel in Mumbai after a long, dusty, bumpy bus ride from Jodhpur. Maya had, hours before, fallen into an ill-temper after an Indian man on the bus had attempted to fondle her leg. Aside from the fact that Maya loved her solo travel time that trip and then hated traveling with Lorna almost immediately. She had failed to measure the depth of Lorna's aggravating tendencies before agreeing.

She saw it as a clear intrusion of her mind and a vexation. She found time with Lorna quickly became a haranguing verbal mess of Lorna's bossy, un-fun ideas and nasal, whiny, well, rather *Waspy* voice. She was teetering on hate. It happened in a heart beat.

Maya was learning her very first lessons in discernment with humanity at this time, the way we all do between about 18 and 25 years of age. The whole time, and for years after she could not get past something that had happened.

She reclined on the bed to read while Lorna showered. This was subsequent to their arrival and entry into the hotel, Lorna resultantly using most of the minimally- supplied hot water. Maya had needed to pee. Maya waited until her cohort was done preening and then went into the bathroom. Mid-pee, she glanced over to the sunlit window sill. There, enshrouded in late evening light and bird song, she saw her requisite hair-cutting scissors, ones she had packed to use to trim her own long, wild, curly head of hair during the trip. (This was essential to Maya's sanity, as it grew like weeds and got in her face, so needed maintenance almost weekly) There they were, sitting on the counter, taken right out of her cosmetics bag.

With Lorna-coloured mousy pubic hair all over them.

And then there were the girls Maya had gone to university with. These were high school associates of Lorna's, ironically. Poseurs, indeed. Birds of a feather…They had their hippie clothes on, but clearly they, too, had come from families of wealth, families who helped them every step of the way with university funding. Oh, the combination of rich ironies: they wore the uncomplicated rags of a Buddhist, while they drove SUV's, smoked Camels, slept with one another's boyfriends and gossiped in evil tones about their 'friends', all the while smiling to their faces. These musings chapped Maya's hide no end and she felt an unrestrained ire growing in her as she remembered the ways of her own petty homeland. The injustice!

While Maya sat, attempting to calm herself of her school week's worth of classroom dramas, learning challenges and teacher bitchiness, she felt a growing pang of aggravation wash over her. She seemed to be angst-ing up, not down as she had very much hoped the library would influence her spirit accordingly.

Was she about to menstruate? Oh, yes, it was drawing close to the full moon, but she could be irritable because she felt over-stimulated most of the time in Guadalajara, without Zach. Oooh, she missed his sex, missed his jokes, missed listening their favourite music together. Having a boyfriend when you really loved the guy was pure bliss. Maya's difficult feelings turned to raw sadness. She felt a lump rising rapidly in her throat. Oh, what a melee of feelings! They weren't subsiding, but growing in latitude in fact! She must be homesick. Damn.

Yet, she needed to work, needed to grow the investment she was making in her career, and she was valued at her school. She decided to just sit there and feel what she felt and not argue with it, or rationalize or make it part of her changing physiology. She was hurt, sad, pissed off.

A good time to write.

From Maya's diary:

Sept.17, Independence Day/2009, Mexico

Hypocrisy

'It seems that where, during my stint at university, taking 'Women's Studies' classes and being an angry feminist was a convenient guise, a safe envelope for unresolved, self-indulgent rage, Buddhism has been hit with the same kind of sheepish hiding of fools recently.

And a fucking major lack of courageousness it is!

Fuck you fucking people: you're angry, so get *mad*. Have it out and be done with it. Don't give it a whole other title, or save it for a rainy day, only to explode on others later. Go off and have that emotion until you've worked it all through. Come back to us and call up your friends to chat and be kind again when you have something worthwhile to say. No one needs to have their own lives-so rife with every day challenges-ruined by anger from anyone else who is pretentious enough to be such a faker. You call yourselves Buddhists, but then you spit tacks at others! You say, 'Namaste' out of one side of your mouth, turn the corner and condemn someone else's life or boyfriend or hairstyle or life choices.

Hypocrites.

That's petty. That's a waste of words, waste of pure space.

It seems duly self-absorbed and very *un*-Buddhist to randomly shoot out venom at unwitting targets. Clearly the message of 'Buddhism' has been re-worked to suit the Unaccountable. The Dalai Lama himself must be in need of a strong gin & tonic at this point, no? Dealing with the misinterpretation of his good message?

Majority of westerners just don't get it. They're incapable. The Tibetans, the Bhutanese, who've traveled across the Himalayas to escape Chinese occupation, running on ice caps in flip-flops, no less, *they* get it. They need such message to even carry on. Imagine.

Even a street bum in California has a better life, an easier time, access to good dumpster dives than those folks.

Honestly!

And then there was Tiffany Simons, who never forgave her mother for sleeping with the gardener and would remain angry for *eternity,* spouting unending diarrhea of her own self-interested rage. She had renamed herself 'Lotus'.

Pleasant.

Our Lotus was no less fuelled by fury and so she converted the message of Buddhism to suit her own heated needs. Damn near annihilated very person in her immediate vicinity verbally, to their faces and behind their backs! The gal became the biggest Buddha Nazi ever. It was super difficult to listen to her at all as time went on.

Special sign over toilet to Lotus:

'Stop shitting all over the universe just because you didn't get enough attention as a child or your dad left.

Better than Buddhism, just another form of extremism as interpreted in the western world in my view, is this bumper sticker they sold at a Dead show in Cal Expo, 1994, when I went with cousin Haya:

'FUCK MORE, BITCH LESS'

Also good: MY KARMA RAN OVER YOUR DOGMA, which I put on my first used vehicle.

Could Tiffany/Lotus be any *less* Buddhist? She used it as her cover, her cloak. A blatant bastardization of the philosophy.

It is so very 'Western' to interpret Buddhism as dogma. I know you, Tiffany. I held parties when my parents went to Napa for the weekend where we all smoked plenty of pot together.

But you pissed me off so much so frequently; I just really need not know you any longer. (Oh dear. Me, a born Jew, going against my own brethren. But is Tiff/Lotus really a Jew if she says she is a Buddhist? An opinionated, mouthy Jew-Bu perhaps?)

In any case, that kind of hypocrisy really gets my goat. (pen marks intense at this junction, depicting an attack of strong emotion)

I want only to know the world's brightest most inspired stars and then nourish those bonds. (heavily underlined in purple sparkle marker)

Good to have my Zach. Maybe it's missing him and the lack of whoopee that is making me so pissed off today. Better go listen to Angie Stone.

As the waiter calmly says in the high-end restaurant, with clear restraint worthy of being Buddhist, 'Very good' once your order is politely taken.

Hell, he didn't even realize he was a living Buddha.'

* * * * * * * *

Maya departed the library, went for a coffee to change the scene. She was brimming. It was not defusing. She sensed the librarian could feel her pounding annoyance and it seemed unfair to have such a degree of slew in her head after all the librarian's likely hard days.

Perhaps the librarian had not been laid in almost 3 months, either.

* * * * * * * *

They had damn good coffee in Guadalajara.

Maya sat and watched people in a tiny art-infused coffee house outside the main drag. Ok, really this was lovely. This was Saturday in Mexico. Come on now. There were gorgeous people everywhere. Gorgeous. Fabulous clothes, better than Italy! Hairstyles of wonder with thick black locks. The kitchen aromas were lovely, cinnamon-y and buttery and golden and goo-od.

She'd chosen a fine spot in which to spectate. As the liquid gold filled her veins, she felt a skip of guilt thinking about how hard the coffee bean pickers had worked, up steep hillsides and vicious embankments to get the goods. Contending with *banditos* at every turn! Scraping hands, legs, feet, backsides on loose hillside branches. Oh, Conscience! Was she just supposed to have guilt along to be able to enjoy everything now? Who knew?

She thought how fortunate she was to be able to sit and enjoy and intellectualize all these floating ideas when those men had to lug close to 70 pounds to the roasters on their bask at the end of the day and sharpen their machetes for the next. No, Maya just could not let go her built-in sense of Guilt.

At least she did not take a drop in the cup for granted. And it had the most wonderful uplifting effect on her. In a matter of half and hour, Maya was moving quickly past being a moaner. She felt inspired to enjoy life! A furtive, caffeine-fuelled second diary entry came upon her in the form of literary celebration on that holiday:

Entertainment: Why We Have our Voices

'Here are some more books I so enjoyed that I would share with others and then we could discuss:

'**The Pearl**' by John Steinbeck. Very powerful short story. Timeless and very perfect for a Mexican foray by a U.S. citizen.

'**11 Minutes**' by Paulo Coehlo. Well-written and a cool interpretation (justification perhaps?) of a young prostitute's life. I liked it.

Everyone should also familiarize themselves with classic (Jewish) mother nuisances like: Infantilizing Your Kids, Being Drunk While Looking One's Best, Favouritism and Scape-goating the daughter by watching '**Arrested Development**'

Other GREAT films:

'**Como Agua para Chocolate' (Like Water for Chocolate)** by Laura Esquivel. My favourite movie *ever*. Have seen 8 times. Want to own.

'**The Water Horse**'. It's a kid's film, starring Emily Watson, but I loved it. It is the story of the Loch Ness Monster. Great for teachers to share with kids or moms and dads to share with Young Einsteins. The baby monster: so cute!

'Shawshank Redemption'. Everyone loves, right?

I was a little bummed that I thought to pack my laptop to keep at my kids' schoolwork marking...but failed to pack my damn power cord. I remembered EVERYTHING today. I just forgot that. Perhaps I was trying subconsciously to give myself a little rest?   Now all I have is diary to write to. Can't even record any more marks for the students. Oh, well. It's *Sabado.*

Biking home now, I think. Use this caffeine high to my advantage. Backbends on the maybe once I get home. Also keen to look at butterflies and go walking as the city sun goes to bed. The town has nice walking off the main drag. I am now friends with all the locals in my 'hood.'

* * * * * * * *

As Maya exited the café, she noticed she was being watched by a scruffy looking young man in skinny jeans and a purple and black top. She had taken to noticing things he had not noticed in the past, things she had once taken for granted in her other life before. The man was of 'Emo' attire and demeanor, not her type at all, possibly even gay. Bi-sexual? She tried to avoid his glance and keep moving. She really didn't need any more male attention after the kind of cat-calls she received routinely walking home from school or going to *tiengues* for her weekend shop.

He persisted in his staring at her, almost making her feel violated. He took his sunglasses off; revealing eyes with mass pupils dilated the size of small coins.

The guy was very high.

Maya turned abruptly and grabbed her locked bike to flee.

He called to her, "Bella! Mi bella!"

She held her head up, kept walking.

'Mi Bella, Preciosa. Tu es en mi corazon, como luz, como paz. Tue ez paz y luz, verdad!'

('My Beauty, Precious. You are in my heart, like light, like peace. You are peace and light, for real')

Very cute.

* * * * * * * *

Chapter 12

Par Ejemplo

'I touch the future: I teach'

—Prologue in a first year university Pedagogical Education manual

Each day, Maya was awakened by church bells and screeching roosters at dawn. These two events happened just before the sun came up. The rooster started his song at about 4:35 am each day. The church bells from Templo San Bernardo sounded out at 4:45 am, and then again on the quarter hour, each hour until noon. After that time, they took a break and waited it out until 4:45 pm, when the bells for Mass began. The nightly church bells went on until 9 pm each day.

It was a celestial greeting, a guaranteed background vocal of Dios and a daily event as respected, needed and understood as the Virgin de Guadalupe whose world-weary eyes were said to cry tears of true blood when her gaze fell upon her followers after the annual 3:00 am Catholic exodus through the outskirts of the city.

Maya had so many different classes to teach, she needed that premature wake up. This gave her time to wash her dishes or her hair as the case may be, write home, plan additional details to integral student lessons or work on supplemental infrastructure needed badly by the school.

Her classes: Special Needs children's program and Honda car factory Business Negotiations ESL classes for adults were run out of the same school where she worked teaching 5th Grade all day each week. Maya was earning the equivalent of $5 US per hour for her vigilant dedication. This came down to about $3.87 after she paid her Mexican civic taxes each paycheque. This was virtual volunteer work.

When Maya had first come to teach at The International School, she had noted there was no special programming for special needs children. She had also noted that disciplinary format ran the gamut from terror tactics used to intimidate the children to outright hitting them on their knuckles with rulers if they were deemed 'naughty'. It actually appeared to her that the whole of Mexico as a country had very little time or patience for anyone with a disability, adult or child. No special services were in place, even in the best private schools, no specialized road access for those in wheelchairs, no ramps. It was as though things had gone back in time in Maya's eyes. It seemed barbaric. People were mean and cruel to anyone who was different or not 100% functional.

It was all quite the opposite with the government and privately-funded Special Needs programs, of which there were plenty in the U.S. She had to keep in mind Mexico is still considered the Developing World. Yet, her conscience had her and she was teaching many with learning challenges. Attention Deficit Disorder, Fetal Alcohol Syndrome/Fetal Alcohol Effects, Obsessive-Compulsive Disorder and Dyscalculia were evident in her classroom every day. She was grateful she'd had so much training in Special Needs education to be able to redirect her own students when necessary, keeping her classes at even keel and getting the best out of each child.

But she was horrified to find the Mexican teachers leaving kids with challenges out in the hallway, lesson after lesson, or punishing them further by being blatantly rude to them, screaming put downs at them or ignoring these children. They did not care and they made no bones about it. The Mexican staff knew these 'tanto' (fools, stupid) children had not an ounce of Hope after graduation-if they even made it past ninth grade. And so a natural malaise descended in other classrooms a lessening of integrity based on the instructor's own jaded, ill-educated perception. Maya felt it was, in truth, sickening. Where were ethics?

It concerned her, as did so many things about the school that appeared to have no explanation or logical basis. Her mind was generating more questions that held no clear answers. This had never worked well for Maya: she was a thinker, a creator, a believer and still an idealist as a teacher. Her vocation was akin to her deeply held beliefs as a woman. Of course, she had the luxury of vast and questioning beliefs as he had grown up with freedom of speech, critical thinking and post-secondary education that may for some in the US go on for 15 - 20 Ivy League years. It was her privileged angle of thought. Not the same angle this country was founded on. It was the angle of the elite North American.

Her go-to person, the International Liaison was scarcely available to help her if she had questions. There were cockroaches and a nest in the bathroom connected to her homeroom, which no one seemed to notice. One of the children in the class got hit at home, and made it clear by coming to school unkempt and with bruises on various parts of his body. Who did she go to ask if this child needed help? At home, she was trained to greet situations of abuse or neglect with appropriate follow-up care for the child, contacting Social Services. Those kinds of supports didn't seem to be available here. Really, her Spanish was not yet so advanced she could just call up the Mexican equivalent of Social Services.

In fact, as Maya looked around, she noted increased weirdness amongst the staff group around her. She picked up on little things, but there were so many of them, the Mexican staff and the picture was getting painted clearer and clearer to her each day. She wondered what kind of qualifications to teach the homeland staff had to hold. They were being paid less than the international staff; they couldn't easily leave Mexico. Did they even have to qualify?

There was so little happening in the way of quality education, Maya made it her mission to bring as much to the school and the children whose lives she impacted daily as she could. She would do her family proud. She would live up to the very best principals of education California had given her, despite working in sub-par conditions. Maya would single-handedly see to it that she touched the future of Mexico through her love of teaching and education.

She was alone in her servitude. It was thankless, invisible. She made two steps forward philanthropically, and observed an immediate landslide backwards. What use was this altruism she'd been raised on amidst brutes like these?

Again, her circumstance begged the question: what was she doing here in this savage place?

She re-wrote the school's Policy on Discipline and made copies for all the staff. She made a hand out on Non-Coercive Education and gave that out at the next staff meeting. When the International Liaison eventually quit due to working far too many unpaid hours, Maya stepped in and took the job, sans pay. When staff called in sick, Maya was there to take their places. Reliable, responsible, solid Maya was how she was viewed by staff, students and parents alike. By her second month at the school, everyone knew her and respected her work. This was no less irritating to her Mexican cohorts. Professional jealousy descended upon Maya like a collective of vultures the moment she faced her disillusionment.

Maya believed in her work and wanted to expand her love of and understanding of her native neighbours in her neighbourhood. She didn't come to change the face of the nation, but it was awfully hard to identify the ethical fiber she was finding, increasingly, each school day. In the face of this system that seemingly didn't have the good of the child at its center, Maya was eating a full plate of Reality. She had gone beyond basic humble pie.

Maya was no less sensitive to and puzzled by freaky and paranoid behavior she continued to witness on the part of her colleagues. She'd been told the Mexican staff was somehow threatened by some of the international staff the school hired. This was talked about on the playground in hushed tones by Denverites, Californians, New Yorkers and Arizonians who'd also taken leave of the comforts of America to be here this year, under contract. The international staff seemed to change each year, or every second year at the most.

The native Mexicans seemed to keep their jobs, even for what appeared to be less pay and fewer hours. Was anything ever as it appeared here?

Maya, whose mother was an artist, had a well-bred love of visual art. On her Top Ten list even prior to arrival in Guadalajara was to take the underground subway advertised on the *Tourismo Guadalajara* website and then to arrive at the newly finished Guggenheim gallery, which was depicted like a massive oval egg like structure, high up on the edge of the *Baranca*. She was to have her hopes dashed in that first week of exploration when, in all truth, the subway had not been finished in over 9 years and showed no near signs of completion due to missed government funding. The Guggenheim may have appeared in Photo Shop online. It hadn't iterated construction in Guadalajara at all, not even so much as the first foundation being laid! The *Baranca* in it's canyon of birds, plants, trees and arid wildlife, was fit for weddings and *Quincinera* parties for 15-year-old-girls.

The Guggenheim she'd seen could only be seen on the internet.

One woman, Thimbu, meaning 'strong dominant one' certainly wanted Maya to have a miserable year. She went to painstaking efforts to ostracize Maya, making her feel small and ensuring she would have a lousy time. She spread false rumours about the Californian teacher, undermined her work ethic to cohorts and students alike. She lied about Maya.

Maya tried to manage it as her father would: by asking objective questions. When Maya looked at 'Bu-Bu' as she was called for short closely, why did it seem like the woman was in such poor health? She had wild eyes. Maybe psychosis? And Big Bu was prone to bouts of crying or screaming publicly. Most uncouth. Was it something as superficial as that Maya was pretty and nimble as Bu-Bu was ugly as the back end of sewer and wicked to boot?

Maya had never really understood deeply mean people. It took so much energy to be that angry. So much planning of ill-thoughts, sucking of joy, countering of progress. She did not see the light. Objectivity was mired in Maya's deficit of comprehension.

If Bu-Bu was in a bad mood, God forbid the child that stood in the hallway. She was utterly savage, terrifying as a personality. It made Maya further sick to her core. While Maya loved to teach, this was all just way too unfamiliar. Her tolerance for the way things were done was emerging into a lowered state by the minute.

* * * * * * * *

It was a P.E. day that Wednesday morning, which would give Maya just enough time to run up to Copy Royale on Chapultepec to have her Chinese New Year celebration masks laminated for her students. She could even grab a special treat: an authentic Earl Grey tea at Starbuck's, one block before she reached the copy place. It was becoming a ritual part of the Mexican decent into winter. Guadalajara, being an inland, higher elevation city, actually had a winter. It grew chillier by the evening and many locals donned caps and scarves with full winter coats. It was milder than a Midwestern winter in the U.S., of course, but it wasn't the *playa* by any means.

Maya was on a brief break while the students had P.E. She gathered her bag and her sunglasses as the children went outside to start their game of volleyball. As she exited, she caught site of Juan, Octavio's father.

'Oh, hola, Juan. You must be here with Octavio's homework?' Maya asked him in Spanish.

'No, *en verdad*, I uu-uh…' Juan stammered, momentarily unable to hold it together. Beautiful, almost as lovely as his wife, direct, intelligent, fresh Maya energy beamed his way. She was classically lovely as a teacher, a California Jewish hybrid, the most alluring kind. At first Juan's pheromones mingled with hers in the musty air of the front hallway of the school. This caught him off guard.

Maya felt nothing of the sort in return, yet she sensed Juan's *machismo*, another turn off to her. She was a pragmatist and would never involve herself with a married man. She found Juan unattractive aside from the base facto that she held no interest in pushing boundaries of professionalism as a teacher. She missed Zach and that was all.

He real couldn't afford to be off guard that day. Juan was standing in the front hall of his child's school holding a kilo package of cocaine that had been wrestled into tiny blue balloons ready for transport via a mule in his arms. Hence, he was now sweating with below-the-belt sensations, combined with some good strong Catholicism-infused Guilt in his son's school's front hall. This was the agreed drop off point, where Bettos would be taking the package via Sergio to have it successfully moved down the highway, out of Puerto Vallarta, onto a plane, to be sold again at a higher amount on Northern Coastal shores.

Juan needed to get his game on and fast. Maya was observing yet more baffling weirdness, she was sure of that, but was having difficulty putting her finger on what she felt. Naturally she had never tried cocaine and had zero interest in the substance. Her head was going more to late tuition fees? A forgotten lunch for his little terror?

'I uu-uh…um, I came to pay Octavio's tuition', he managed to shoot back to Maya as a weak cover, though not as quickly as he would have liked.

'Oh, I see. Of course,' Maya replied, looking him right in the eyes. Maya noticed a blackhead above his right brow. How unseemly.

She wasn't buying this at all.

'Actually, now I have you here, Juan, I'm going to need to set a meeting with you and Elisa to talk a little about Octavio's behavior in the classroom. He's been having a tough time in class, as well as out on the school yard. I think we should talk about where your son is at.' She said, pointedly and without backing down. As big a sweetheart as Maya was, she was verbally direct when she needed to be.

This scenario was taking away from others in her classroom and needed to be handled without delay.

Maya had the strong workaholic tendencies of her father, so she didn't have to hold this sacred time as her own. Her tea could wait and she still had enough time to have the masks laminated. Every student's success in her class was tantamount.

'Oh, ok. *Si, chido,* ' (slang for 'cool') Elisa and I will call the school to arrange a suitable meeting time, Ms. Maya. Thank you.' Juan was itching to get out of the school. He felt so odd, unusually clammy and unnerved in front of Maya. He was sure she knew something; sure she could see right through him. He felt his shoulder rise a little on his left side.

He was so good at being cool, calm, collected most times; this physiological reaction was quite unusual for the man. That was why Juan's role was generally ensuring deliveries, one of the more dangerous and difficult parts of the Narco Traficante route.

It was as if Maya had seen into him, he thought as he stumbled out the front, not sure where to go next, the devious package still in hand. She had spoken so directly. She could see why his son might be having trouble in her class, Juan sensed that. Paranoia was clouding his mind, only aggravating him further. Had he done too much of the good stuff at Bettos' last night? She wasn't about to stand for anything less than the full application of her students. Yet, Juan knew he simply hadn't bred young Octavio that way.

Maya, still present in the issue at hand, was fine with a meeting, but she would hound the family if this display proved he was only saving face. She was used to the normal circuitous journey many of her students' families took in saving face. If the situation was unacceptable, they would craft intricate stories or make 'false arrangements', even lunches or dinners that would never truly come to be in order to vague-ify their goings one. At first, this had bothered Maya, who found it insulting to behave so transparently. Maya's own family in California were all about just getting it out on the table, butt-ugly details and all.

She couldn't fathom this bizarre need to save face, but here it was.

Maya was trying her best to move away from the comforting thoughts of her own familiarity 'back home' to assimilate here. She would have to in order to survive this entire teaching contract, so as not to let her students down. She was adapting.

She had grown used to it from some, but she dared not be disrespectful to Juan. Maya was aware that he was on the Board of the school. Perhaps he would see to it that they get a wheelchair ramp for Sofia who so badly needed it, or that Chayo, in the mediocre school cafeteria, was given a higher budget for menu planning.

'Gracias, Señor.' Maya said to Juan, not one to paint things as rosy if they were grave. 'Clarity will be good and then we can decide what the best road is for Octavio in the meeting.' She was out the door, on her way to quick errands on her break before she would return to class.

Maya pushed out of the gate and went on up the street, enjoying the breezy palms and birds singing down the length of Libertad en route to the main street.

* * * * * * *

Chapter 13

Regalos

'We should give as we would receive, cheerfully, quickly, and without hesitation;

for there is no grace in a benefit that sticks to the fingers.'

–Seneca

Elisa felt she was being sidelined from Juan's life. If she had learned one thing as a young fugitive from her own family, it was the power of observation. Not that her family ever came after her as she'd very much hoped someone related to her by blood would do, but she had become a highly perceptive human being as a result.

As much as perhaps Elisa didn't need the gory details of the deaths Juan was involved with, nor the rip-offs, pay offs and scores of scams, she did like to know at least where he was going. She liked to touch base with her husband-an understandable and bona fide human sentiment.

Lately, she was being left out of these specifics. No matter how she tried to love him, he was distancing himself from her and most definitely from their dear Octavio. This was taken to dramatic proportions in the wild heart of Elisa and became an arousing stumbling block for the Narco wife. She was hurt and saddened and very pissed off.

That afternoon, she decided it was time to go shopping for some nice *regalos* (gifts) to fill her consign of pain. She would not be left all alone, a feeling she'd been born into and was desperate to move far far away from. She would not be abandoned again. She would become visible to Juan again if she was so invisible.

She prepared a list for Sofia. She seemed to indulge in working Sofia even harder than the elderly maid usually worked when Elisa was angry. Sofia was quite used to this. It was a part of her job and she dutifully kept on her list of tasks. Sofia was in no place to risk anything.

She hopped in the SUV ML 500 Mercedes and roared off to Plaza de Gallerias, a US-inspired mall not far from what she'd seen on television in the construction of Ft. Worth, Texas. An air-conditioned movie, a shot of tequila, a decadent lunch, a bag of real Mexican chocolates, a new pair of shoes to showcase a perfect pedicure and a blow out at the salon were in order. Juan could foot the $1660 pesos bill. She felt better already.

* * * * * * * *

Maya was nearing the end of her school day. She noticed Paolo, one of her most attentive students usually, was sitting very quietly. She went to him as her students were finishing up their projects for the day.

"Paolo, do you want to walk over to the office with me? I have to pick up some copies for tomorrow's lessons." Maya asked him in a hushed voice.

He looked up at her, on the verge of tears.

"Yes, Teacher. I do."

Maya nodded and he got up. She went to the front of the room and asked Isaac if he would please lead the group for 3 - 5 minutes in the completion of their assignments. She expected all the work to be wrapping up by the time she and Paolo returned from their errand. Isaac, normally a little monkey in school for most of his previous teachers, loved Maya. He, like his cohorts called her, 'Miss Maya'. He was very happy to have been given some responsibility and would not let her down. She believed in all her kids; she trusted that.

Paolo and she slipped out of the room. He asked if he could hold her hand. She took his clammy little hand and looked at him. He was shaking and looked like the tears were about to burst.

"What is it, *Mijo (young dear one)*?" she asked, concerned for Paolo, her blossoming classroom artist.

"Teacher, I am sad. My mama and papa have not time for me. They are so busy; they leave me alone so much. And the only one I have is my Grandpa, but he's about to die."

Maya had seen many gifts in Paolo. He had started out the school year with her a bit shaken up, it was clear. He'd had some issues concentrating on his Math and Spelling/Pronunciation of English was a genuine challenge for Paolo. But Maya taught with an open heart and a big sense of humor, often joking about her own deficits and making her pupils feel at ease. Within a few weeks for their year together, she was witnessing young Paolo rounding a corner and having unremitting success. He was most especially gifted in art, whipping up creations the like of which she had never seen before. She cared for this boy and wanted him to leave school for the day feeling good again.

"Paolo, my good man. I know life gives us a lot that we find hard to manage. But, you have many gifts and a very fine mind. Sometimes, mama's and papa's have a lot to take care of to make a good life happen for their children. Could it be that your mama and papa are really just busy providing for you?"

By this time, fat tears were rolling down Paolo's cheeks.

"Yes, ok, but I feel like I never get any time with them. I want to ask for just an afternoon to talk and be with them. You say it is because they care. I feel like it is because they are bored with me."

"Well, trust me. They care. You should do just that-ask them. Why not organize a family picnic for you and your brother, mama, papa and grandpa?"

"Teacher, I can do that, yes," Paolo said in his think accent. "But I am still angry."

"I know. That anger comes from your feeling disappointed. You need to be a big person here and try to make it different. Use your gift-your mind-and all your creativity to do that, Paolo. Most of the families I know in America have a time challenge, too. It happens often. As we get older, we see that time is worth more than money."

"Well, Miss Maya, I will try, but not for them, only because you asked me to," the boy said, still hostile and not understanding that this situation had far less to do with him and more to do with the general lack of *dinero* that is a very real part of life in Mexico.

Maya chuckled. "Great that you want to do this to inspire. But you do this for <u>you</u>, for your people, not for me, Paolo. Do this for the sake of making a solid change or at least letting your family know how you feel. Do this because you love them not because you're mad at them, Paolo."

Paolo couldn't help but smile with his teacher as they came around the corner to the office. He loved Miss Maya and he wanted to show her what a big strong good man he was.

Maya collected her copies, thanking Alicia, one of the prettiest women Maya had ever seen.

They returned to the classroom. Isaac had done well. The class was finishing up calmly, putting their hard work on her desk to be marked for the next day. Maya had her own gift with children; she could see the pearl inside each of these amazing young people. That in itself was enough to keep her motivated, against all odds by this point.

And a gift she needed. Maya was being beleaguered by regular stomach upsets and loneliness at night before she slept. She knew something was rotten in the state of Denmark; something about this place was just not right. Something about everything here was not right. Her senses were up but she felt blind to the cause.

Maya needed some kind of sign to pull her through. The bell rang, with the children dismissed, many hugging her on the way out the door. She could breathe a sigh of relief that she was fulfilling her career intention helping them grow and learn. Surely, this would go down as a good school year for them at closing of the term. Maya would see it through, even if she was pained with homesickness, missing Zach, her own family and her sense of self.

The struggle to gain insight had led her to see that for her, it was daily familiarity that bed content. That and she was damned tired of how she felt around some of the people she had to be around at school. Where she was from, community made humanity: people worked together. She had not seen females in particular behave in this regressed way since she was in second grade.

One has to pick one's battles. Who needed this noise? Sick of trying source it out, Maya was sure she could wrap her mind around more worthy topics.

* * * * * * * *

And so it was: Maya experiencing countless feelings that afternoon, Elisa with her own heart full. Each woman motivated entirely differently, each wrestling with disappointments of their own.

Maya walked over to her bike with her backpack full of work. She would ride home through the downtown core, just to look again at the light pink cowboy *botas* (boots) with the striking embroidery up the side of them. Just to buy Copal incense for her living room while she marked, just to see a little taste of distraction before she ended that day.

As she approached Centro, traffic was stalled for two city blocks. In a city the size of Guadalajara, with its multiple circuits and alleys ways and one-way streets, this was caus8ing quite a commotion during perpetual rush hour. Maya was curious.

She biked towards the town square, where there were often artists with handsome designs selling or unique books or lively musicians filling the air with passion. This time, right outside McDonald's, there was a stand giving out free tacos with a sign on it, "Verdad Mexico" (real Mexico). Jalisco, the state Guadalajara sat in was renowned for its beef production.

There were 3 people running the booth and plenty of takers. In strong Spanish voices they were saying, '*This* is our food, the food of our land. This is real fast food, pure in health and the best you can get for mere pesos. McDonald's is our neighbour's version of food. It is not real food; it can hurt your body! Come enjoy what your land has given us for eons. Don't let us be sold out to the US. Don't let us be taken!'

While the calm comfort of familiarity was breeding a mounting hunger in Maya, and she missed a lot about home, this was beautiful. It was true. Her family had been very leftist in their approach. Likely, it was this questioning of Truth that led Maya to posit so many questions. She was not raised on processed foods and had no taste for McDonald's.

Maya had come here to see what Mexico was up to, to see progress of this sort. Guadalajara held many educated people, a strong political vein and was prone to protest, controversy and government lobbying. It was a university-fuelled city and had enough culture, global awareness and sheer brain power in its mignons to ensure that the questions that Mexico needed to ask were being asked. All the while, it housed more drugs and corruption than even Bush could shake a stick at.

The apparent juxtaposition of politics in both Mexico and her cherished US fell upon Maya. Neither nation was blind to their realities. Maya was taking the wool off her eyes through experience.

She took the image with her as she biked away from the crowd scene. It had touched her, alit her inner maverick. She'd known only the more typical beachy, surfy Mexico in the past. Puerto Escondido, with its vibrant art scene and night life had entertained her on Spring Break in the past.

She'd assumed Mexico was unaware in her youth's ignorance. How wrong she was. The kind of political demonstrations that Guadalajara was renowned for were new to her.

The world outside the US was finding more voice, through bumps and wiggles unique to each cause.

Maya took palpable gifts of intellect with her that afternoon in Mexico.

Zach's hands would be doing the right things to her in less than 32 hours. It was a good day.

No one would return with empty pockets that day.

* * * * * * * *

Chapter 14

Descoubrir

'There came a time when the risk to remain tight in the bud

was more painful than the risk it took to blossom.

-Anaïs Nin

Juan looked at Alicia, the secretary at the front with Aztec blood roots. Alicia had to be part of The Family, as Sergio referred to members of the staff Who Knew. She had to identify who needed to be contacted in the receipt of certain transfers, as well as making up school bus passes. This knowledge she held near her breast also afforded her a steady job, enough to feed her daughters and her husband, who was chronically out of work and even more chronically into smoking *potacion*.

Alicia had felt Juan's discomfort in front of Maya. The Mexican staff group were growing annoyed with The U.S. transplant, as they all felt she upended them in how hard she worked for that school. The regressed among us hate change most times. Alicia looked at Juan, as Maya flew out the door, her eyes widened. Juan took a deep breath and let out a sigh of relief. If Maya was going to be promoted to Principal next year, she would eventually need to know. He was pretty sure a solid cash grab on a regular basis would keep her quiet, as it did effectively with the others who knew.

Alicia said, 'Here, Juan, give it to me and I will page Bettos right away.' She knew by its size and the evident shaking in Juan's hands how much he was holding. She had seen Juan for deliveries and 'late tuition payments' for Octavio since Octavio had been in Kinder at the age of four.

'Oh, Alicia. I think she knows. I feel so strange, *mala onda* (bad vibe)' Juan replied, uncharacteristically shaken by the incident.

'We can make her understand. Don't worry,' Alicia replied, with deft calm, the manufactured kind, going back to her filing.

* * * * * * *

Maya went to free her mind into her journal. A moment of realization, Zen-like, had come upon dear Maya, as she stared up at the dangling viney jungly boulevard on Libertad outside her school. It was moment of enduring classic Mexican beauty. The street was movie-worthy, so pretty. She was having her first real touch of the freedom that comes with learning about other people a little more. Not unlike the freedom of a first orgasm or the freedom a hummingbird has in its sheer haste.

She wished for tequila that minute, but got over it fast. Should not be drinking while at work. That was absurd. Yet, she felt compelled to Bacchus.

Alas, he writing would have to suffice as a form of venting for now. She gave her little missives a title, even in her diary. Teaching was at least partially ingrained in the woman. While she titled her entries, she also gave way to drawings of mirth or satire in the margins and a colloquial use of grammar.

Full Moon, Dec. 23/2009, Guadalajara

December, 2009

Dreams

'Tonight, in the still-here sunlight, we're going out in the boat. $400 used aluminum skiff. Better investment than cable TV, I see Zach again, in my dreams. I see us, with a picnic and a joint that came down from San Fran and our favourite songs. I am just remembering and I feel so much.

I have boundaries. I believe the combo of coming to a new very different country than my own, with no language skills save 11th Grade leftover Spanish has brought about a better woman. I am sure trying here…doing my own homework consistently and being fastidious about 'personal housekeeping' is helping me maintaining them almost effortlessly.

Sadly, most others don't. They don't go deeper than what is in front of them. And they admit they don't care to. That bugs me. I don't really want that near me. Sheer laziness.

Thing is, boundaries are worth it. I do feel I take a much more critical eye to my life now. Perhaps it's because I see myself as a journalist-teacher before Fall. Maybe it's falling in love with Zach. It could be just plain growth. What I am living solo in Mexico is no bottomless Margarita, let me tell ya.

I am doing away with 'Low-Return Friendships.'

I have enough assholes in my life through no choice of my own.

Now that my boundaries are what they are, I have self-esteem of a normal and balanced level and I am in a happy, stable, calm, no-drama relationship with the Zach Man, I can't take what I used to.

I look close up at a person who is head-butting my boundaries and I want to get away. I am repelled, in fact.

My perspective has changed: 180 degrees at least.

I guess in previous times I was just glad to have any friends, so was less than discerning.

Now, I *have* to be discerning; there is no question. I have to be.

My male friendships, conversely, are all 'Very High Return', and have the added bonus selection of being 'Humour-Filled, Drama-Free'! *All* of them, without question; sometimes surprisingly and delightfully so.

I have no male friends in my life that I hang with often that I am resentful of. Conversely, too many women I have known over the years annoy the crap out of me. Only the enduring truly rad women, the Goddess SuperAwesomnesses are my longtime friends.

Can I ask these two questions, Diary, my pal:

Once you and your guy decided on one another, did you have waaaa-ay less time for others...and then only want to be with the Very Best when being social?

Is it normal and part of the iterate process of life to need to do some very real downsizing, sometimes a few times a decade? I find I cannot be bothered any longer with folks who are rude, angry, bitchy, petty, lazy, spoiled, unproductive, whiny, self-absorbed or otherwise just 'stuck' in their lives. To me, it appears that is regressed. I see those folks as 'Emotionally Behind.' As an 'Emotional Progressive', I want the Hell away from that shit. I simply will not put up with that.

I have to love and give to my art and my man. And that's about all I really have time for on top of my already-full life. I may be left with very very few pals, but I don't seem to care.

This has helped me a lot with these lousy bitches I have to work with. Weird-ass mean bitches. And, who cares in the end?

I figure, when there are fabulous, amazing people to hang with, why hang with the under-developed? It's too frustrating, not to mention downright boring.

The flip side, which is entirely possible, is that I have turned into a cold-hearted bitch that only has time for The Worthy. Which, in effect, means perhaps I am now A Snob?

Better yet: Frankly, my dear, I don't give a damn!'

* * * * * * *

Maya was going to meet Zach's plane.

* * * * * * *

Chapter 15

Espero

Because I could not stop for Death–

He kindly stopped for me–

The Carriage held but just Ourselves–

And Immortality.'

-Emily Dickinson, from 'Because I Could Not Stop for Death, circa 1863

Gustavo had some explaining to do, as the sunrise hit Ana Lisa's mirror that morning. She was checking her hairline, and rearranging it as she did each day so that the scar didn't show. She was leaving a cheap hotel, where Ana Lisa had been servicing a client. He was sound asleep and she had had enough of his snoring. The girl let herself out, taking the man's cigarette lighter on her way out: a memento for her trouble. At 14, Ana Lisa was so sick of sex, she would be happy if she never had it again.

She had her hair in place and was on her way across the square to Gustavo's tiny room, up a long flight of miniature stairs. Ana Lisa arrived to find Gustavo in a ball, curled up in rags in the corner. It was rare that she was up before him, but he had needed some extra sleep.

'Goose! Goose!' she called to him, walking over to the little lump to rouse her friend. Where have you been, you little tiger? I've been frantic, looking for you!'

Gustavo was somewhere between sleep and waking, not quite ready to face the day. He tried to push her away, turning uncomfortably to face the wall to allow himself a mite more rest. He knew once she was there, she would not leave.

'Mmm-mnnnnnooo' he murmured back at her.

'Gustavo. Wake up now. I want to talk to you.' She persevered.

Gustavo had no choice but to shake the sleep out of his eyes. He would face his last day in the city until night fell with Ana Lisa. He must tell her of his good fortune.

'Ana Lisa, I had a good meal last night. I have a new friend.' Gustavo told her, with naive love light shining in his eyes.

'What happened? I missed you!' She replied

'I got caught up with this guy, Bettos, who has offered me a fair price to go to L.A. I can do it. It's quick and easy'. I've never been to L.A.!' the words came tumbling out of his hopeful mouth. He was so excited, he could hardly get the story straight.

'Gustavo, in your dreams. Whatever. I don't believe you' Ana Lisa replied a bit belligerently.

'Yes, yes, let me tell you', and so he began with the story that Bettos had given him over the most delicious dinner the night before.

Ana Lisa was transfixed, naturally. Every street urchin in Guadalajara is looking for an exit, any kind of Hope.

As the sun set on the burgeoning young dreams of the grubby street children, another glass was raised for a toast in Italy, after a rail was snorted, not far from the Ponte Veccio, as a line was cut up inside the toilet of a nightclub in London, England and handed to a party-goer for nasal ingestion in Paris, France.

Gustavo told Ana Lisa of the story he would live the next day, the many meals he would enjoy, the trip he would take by truck to the airport in Puerto Vallarta.

Ana Lisa had been fed a crock by the patron she'd entertained the night before. He had tried to ply her with stories of wealth and fancy parties, too. She knew she could stomach a few more nights with the fool, but when his child's photo, in a shady glen outside their Connecticut residence fell out of his wallet onto the cheap hotel floor, Ana Lisa had seen enough to know the only light she would see would glisten off a handful of pesos that would be hers as night fell. Ana Lisa counted Hope in days or weeks. That was all she had learned was hers, living the way she had.

Ana Lisa, as much as she wanted to buy Gustavo's dreamy painted picture, knew there would be a horrible other side. Her homeland Mexico was always doing that to her, rubbing her face in her own difficult plight: giving her images of beauty, colour, musical deluges. And then, once she was all wrapped up in enjoyment, butting cigarettes out on her arm.

Gustavo had sold his disbelief down the river he once glimpsed an oasis in the form of escaping the street. He was on his way to the coast already, on his way to find his own version of Hope.

* * * * * * * *

On her way to the store to get cream for their dark coffee that morning, at 7:13 am, Maya was replaying the previous night's live soccer game at Stadio Jalisco with Zach: Argentina vs. Guadalajara's Chivas. It was a heated game, full of obnoxious jeers on the part of Mexico. Apparently there was quite a rivalry between the two teams, almost bordering on racism, it seemed. The Mexican fans yelled 'Punta!' every time an Argentinean player fouled or fell down. The Argentineans for their part weren't helping matters so much by lying on the ground, *crying* and pounding their fists every time they lost a goal. Maya had been lost in the sheer over-the-top beer garden, finding many a local cute she'd never do otherwise without beer goggles on. She rounded a corner.

Yikes! Zach was finally beside her. What the Hell was she thinking? Edit that thought.

At 7:15 am, a bit further along her route that morning, Maya was affronted with a corpse, fresh blood oozing from it, yellow ribbon cordoning off the area it lay in, just in front of Ochenta y Ocho, a grandiose restaurant on Vallarta Avenue.

A photographer leaned in close to get a face shot of the results of a Narco deal gone bad: 17 bullet holes in the face after apparent attempted strangulation. Enough to break any mother's heart, enough to ruin a wife for good.

* * * * * * * *

Chapter 16
Milagro

'Miracles are the retelling in small letters of the very same story

which is written across the whole world

in letters too small for some of us to see.'

-C.S. Lewis

From Maya's diary, upon the regular visitation of stray cats, most particularly an insistent pregnant chocolate/seal point Siamese she'd named Cool Blue:

Kitty in Strife

'Here's a tale that amazed me...Life is one circuitous journey!

OK, I am not sure how I managed it, but I suppose we draw from reserves we didn't even know we had some days. The days we need to be Superheroes.

I didn't study Spanish formally, only I went to *Escuela de Calle* (School of the Street). Well, OK, I took Spanish in both high school and university for 1 year each, but it was really only grammatical structures, no slang, as is used LOTS, and you need conversation/*verbo* conjugations skills to get by in real life. That was some time back. I don't really remember it all.

I have a temporary solution. I listen attentively to *everything* I hear in Spanish on the street. I read 1 page of my Spanish-English dictionary every day, over my morning *Torrificada* dark Mexican roast. Somehow, I can speak Spanish now; I can even tell little *brohmas* (jokes).

The dear little Cool Blue kitty had shown up about 10 weeks back. I named her after the Joan Armatrading song; it fits her pretty eyes. She looks like a purebred and she loves a love-in, so I am not sure if she was always stray, or if she was once somebody's baby and then abandoned over time. Babies, dogs, children have often been attracted to me. There's really no saying why. And street people have heeded the sign on my forehead that reads, LUNATIC MAGNET. They have often approached me randomly, seemingly out of nowhere. (Jesus complex?) Always, if a person seems lost in my midst, they will walk over to me. Like it or not, that's just how it is.

Anyhow, what a personality! All Siamese have that tenacious 'meow' and they can be very dang stubborn. It was as if she came to me saying, 'Listen, Sistah. Life sucks for me right now. Some asshole street cat bonked me-and it hurt like a bitch. I made a ton of noise and so did he. Then, he took off and no one in this *colonia* (neighbourhood) has even seen him again. Sure enough, I found myself knocked-up, my DNA-fed neuroses in overdrive, unable to care for 6-7 burgeoning kittens, hungry as Hell.'

Cool Blue endeared herself to me. She got 10 weeks of loving from me and awesome organic food, of course. It was time to find a place for her to be safely. How to do this with such minimal language skill-or certainly not enough to negotiate a home for her? It had been central in my thoughts, though I didn't know where to begin.

I stepped out of school on Friday, thought about how I can improve my Spanish with such little time off to study. These 57-hour workweeks are nuts, but my school *beg* me to take on even more hours! (I will not at this point. I can't.). I felt ready to either pass out or have a hot bath. Neither were available, and my bike is broken from practicing too many tricks, so I knew I had a LONG walk home in the heat.

Walked about 2 blocks and looked down at something bill-sized on the sidewalk. Could it be? It was a $500 pesos nota! That's about the equivalent of $47 U.S. Who ever heard of finding that much cash on the sidewalk? I have never found that much cash back home, in the Developed World lying on the street. And this is a place where $ is seriously scarce!

I figured it must be a gift from *Dios*. I saw all of it coming together. A few weeks back, I had pulled my broken language skills together enough to begin the process of finding a home for a pregnant cat here, in a landscape where cats are oft hated and many folks are scared of them actually! I know, weird. In a country where most work 10 - 15 hours per day for teeny tiny wages, no one really has the luxury of unfortunate street cat rescues.

I found Ana, The Cat Lady, after quite a search. What a gem! She is going to help here. She'll adopt Cool Blue, assist her in delivery and help her kittens find homes. I will use that $500 pesos to set Blue up with vaccinations, *anti-parasito's* and the little love will have to be checked out for STD's/Herpes, seeing as she was bonked by a savage urchin, matted up in street cat dreads, filthy from survival.

Unbelievable really.

Just as a curve ball smacks you in the face, you get a nice fat piece of chocolate cake.'

* * * * * * * *

Zach had arrived. They spent every moment loving each other, having great sex, going salsa dancing because he knew she loved it and eating the best food Guadalajara had. She took him to Tianguis Cultural. They saw Ballet Folklorico. It was the very best of Guadalajara, with the best man she knew.

They laughed together, eating Garfield's Burgers, near the Oxxo store, off Plan de San Luis that evening as the sun sunk down into its purple-pink Mexican divan. They were the most amazing burgers either of them had eaten-ever. Large enough to leave a person very full, dripping with yummy sauces, and *crema* (a classic Mexican topping, like sour cream, but more liquid-y) and cheese, all the fixings.

For a moment in time, they had paradise. He would fly out again in 21 hours.

Chapter 17

Testamiento

"Your daily life is your temple and your religion.

Whenever you enter into it take with you your all.

Take the plough and the forge and the mallet and the lute,

the things you have fashioned in necessity for delight.

For in reverie you cannot rise above your achievements

nor fall lower than your failures."

-Kahlil Gibran, from "The Prophet", circa 1923

The time had finally come for vacation. A whole 3 weeks. Maya had already seen so much in such a short time, it felt like she had been away for years. She didn't celebrate much of anything, but she was good and ready for some time off school. She planned to fly back into L.A., where Zach was going to meet her at the airport. She was so ready to see her guy and had missed everyone, everything familiar back home. It was a good day. She had 1 more hour to go on the bus out of Guadalajara to the coast and she would be round the corner from the airport. Perfect. She was on her way home.

Gustavo was seated behind Maya's bus on the highway, in a truck that was being driven by a man Gustavo did not know. Bettos was in the seat beside him. He had his head up against the glass and was peeking out at the banana plantations they passed on the sunny winding highway. He had never seen bananas growing on trees before.

Juan had the goods in a separate car, his own Range Rover, navy blue, with tinted windows. He would greet the truck that had Bettos, Gustavo and the mystery driver in it before he escorted the boy to the airport gate.

Elisa was home, getting her clothes on for the gym. Octavio was in Karate class, staring out the window, wondering where his dad had gone to this week.

Ana Lisa was pulling her underwear on, busy feeling nothing.

It was another day in Mexico that had begun with the rooster's crow and the church bells ringing.

Maya turned on her iPod so she could roll into the Puerto Vallarta bus depot thinking about Zach and the love he would be making to her that night. Zach knew how to rock his woman. He was Maya's porn star. She cranked Kings of Leon, 'Milk'.

Gustavo heard Michael Jackson on the radio and tried to sing along with 'ABC'. He had understood that Michael Jackson had died suddenly by reading it in the newspaper. That must have been why they kept playing a lot of his songs ands talking about his being such a 'good man', 'The King of Entertainment' after his passing, June 25, 2009.

Yet, Gustavo remembered a time when the other street kids were insulting one another they would use the term 'MJ' for a person who failed to find his own food and kept trying to take it from other children. Once a person died, it seemed to Gustavo, they became golden. They were getting closer and closer to the airport. Gustavo was about to get on his first airplane.

Juan was listening to Deepak Chopra to try to tone his breathing. He was inhaling for a count of four, and exhaling for a count of six. He was already thinking about getting this delivery onto the plane via the new mule and what he needed to tee up for next week. It was Juan's second border run in a month. No wonder his kid wasn't focusing in school. Juan realized with a tinge of regret that he had not made any special time for his son in a few weeks. He would be in debt to his boy for a trip to the arcade at Gallerias-pronto.

Maya felt the state of vacation dreaming, thoughts of vodka, lime and soda and her favourite bubble bath products fall upon her. She was beginning to let go of the school's shoddy policy-making. Her co-worker's random behaviour. She was so looking forward to seeing her dad.   She wondered if Zach had cut his hair. She was falling asleep to the hum of the bus.

* * * * * * *

Chapter 18

Nervioso

'Worry never robs tomorrow of its sorrow,

it only saps today of its joy.'

Leo Buscaglia

Gustavo could see the runway. 'Up up and away!' he said as they turned into a private driveway, just before the entrance to the airport parking area. About two minutes after they turned into the driveway, Juan's navy Range Rover pulled in behind them. Gustavo had never met Juan.

All the men in the area turned off their cell phones. Gustavo could hear a seagull scream, swooping into the ocean for its prey. It was quiet except for the traffic rush outside.

Juan approached Bettos. The two men stood close to one another and whispered back and forth for a few minutes. Gustavo was still excited, but his street sense began to catch up with him. He felt he needed caution. Something stirred in his belly.

He watched every detail, trying to place information he needed. He knew he had not heard the whole story yet, but all he could think about was going to L.A., seeing Hollywood movie stars everywhere and having food and money. The excitement overtook him.

Juan gave a bag to Bettos. Bettos opened the bag and counted out eight blue bullets. These bullets were about the size of an average woman's thumb. Bettos walked towards Gustavo with the bullets. The bullets were made by forcing as much cocaine as possible into the fingers of blue latex gloves. Once the finger area was full, the stuffed digit was tied off, then cut off, to make a solid-feeling nugget. These bullets were the means by which cocaine traveled by air into the USA.

Gustavo didn't know what was happening. He had not heard this part of the story. He was a tiny boy, in a stranger's truck, hoping for another meal.

Bettos told Gustavo he would need to drink a lot of water, and handed him a bottle of purified Aquafiel. Gustavo was getting hungry and he was more interested in the Coca Cola he'd been promised, upon airport arrival.

'Bettos, can I have a Coca Cola instead?' the child asked.

Bettos knew that the acid in the Coca Cola would be too much for the operation and might cause the bullets to explode and leak. He needed this run to go smoothly for the sake of the entire operation and a successful run. He had little time to play with. He had to steer Gustavo right off the Coca Cola subject.

'No, Gustavo. Coca Cola before a flight is a bad idea.' he replied.

'But, Bettos, you promised!' Gustavo could feel his disappointment. He so wanted a Coca Cola and he had come all this way, over four and a half hours on the highway in this heat.   He wasn't ready to let this go. Now he was realizing his stomach was churning for food, too.

Bettos would not move on it. He stood still and said nothing.

Bettos didn't seem like such a good friend any more.

* * * * * * *

Chapter 19
Escondido

'It is an unfortunate human failing that a full pocketbook often groans more loudly than an empty stomach.'

-Franklin Delano Roosevelt

Maya's bus arrived, with 24 minutes to get her out of the station, and into customs to get on her plane home. The last leg of the journey was getting closer; she had the reminiscence of the tang of the way her dad's homebrew tasted lingering in her mind. She had to get her bag off the bus, full of gifts and treasures she'd found at the antique market and the tienguis (classic Mexican Sunday market) near her home.

As she went down to get her luggage off the bus she caught sight of a man scooting off towards the bathroom. As she looked closer, she realized it was Juan, Octavio's father. She had met with Elisa and Juan the day before the final day of classes in an effort to get some more support from the home front in terms of reading and getting homework assignments done.

'That's funny,' she thought, 'Elisa told me they were staying home for the holidays and that her relatives were coming down from Mazatlan this year. Why is Juan here, I wonder?'

She was quickly distracted by a barking Chihuahua who had broken loose from its owner's leash and was running in frantic circles around the back of the bus.

Juan needed to sprint from the place he'd parked the Range Rover to the airport in order to ensure a safe passage. He gulped a coffee. As soon as he was done scouting the bus station, he was off. He spilled the remainder of the coffee as he dashed away.

* * * * * * *

Chapter 20

Peligroso

'The torment of precautions often exceeds the dangers to be avoided. It is sometimes better to abandon one's self to destiny.'

-Napoleon Bonaparte

Bettos needed Gustavo to swallow the last of the blue bullet capsules and fast. Juan had gone to scout the bus station for cops and use the lavatory. They would proceed to the airport as soon as the last two capsules were gulped. Gustavo would swallow 14 in total. Hard work for a tiny boy not used to this. The process had taken about 20 minutes already, an eternity for a hungry child.

'Come on, Gustavo. No time for games now. This is part of what we need for you to do.'

'But, Bettos, you never told me this part. This is hard. I'm hungry and my throat is getting sore from all this swallowing.' Gustavo complained, his eyes and mind on the Coca Cola that would soon be his.

'Come on!' Bettos urged him, pushing another blue bullet towards him. 'We need you to do this. Now!' he said emphatically.

Gustavo took a deep breath. He downed the last two as quickly as he could.

'They all gone then?' Bettos asked. 'Good then. We gotta run.' He said as he scooped the boy back into the truck and drove like a bat out of Hell the last few minutes to the corner around from the airport.

Gustavo was so hungry, he felt himself slipping again. He was going fast. He needed that Coca Cola.

As Bettos pushed the boy out of the truck, he fell to the ground. Gustavo tried to pick himself up, but Bettos was faster, pulling him up and pushing him to move forward. Bettos' movements changed. He was brusque and cold with the child, not the nice friend who had helped Gustavo when he was so hungry in Centro.

Bettos' job at this point was to ensure he got the signal to go forward to the boarding area with Gustavo from Juan. Juan needed to ensure it was a day free of dogs, undercover cops or suspicious people who hadn't been paid off.

Bettos saw Juan, but there was no signal. He could not move with Gustavo until there was a signal, as he had been instructed. He watched the boy for any signs. He watched Juan intently for a sign. A sign did not come.

* * * * * * *

Maya was brimming with excitement. She moved towards the boarding area. Zach was going to ruffle her hair and tell her he missed her. She was going to be with her family. She was going to eat Ghirardelli's chocolate and eat sourdough bread and real butter go for brunch after Zach and she had stayed in to watch old movies and order Chinese the night before.

Maya was just thinking how good a bath would feel once she was back on American soil, as she turned to see a tiny boy fall down. He crumbled, as if he had exploded.

She looked up at his caregiver, a thin man, who didn't look at all like the boy. 'It couldn't be his father,' Maya thought. 'So where is his mother?'

Juan sprinted across the airport to Bettos and the boy. 'What is he doing here? Why does he look so worried?' Maya wondered. She had just seen Juan at the bus depot. Why was he here now, as well? Maya could not stop herself from staring, compelled.

Juan was trying to help the boy. Bettos was standing still, going white. Maya had no idea who he was. The line was taking forever. Mexico had cultivated a lot of patience in Maya.

* * * * * * *

Maya had only her bag with her and she could not avoid her growing curiosity about Juan and why Octavio's daddy was here without his *familia*. She was drawn to the insolvent child, worried for him. She walked a few steps closer to the sight, losing her place in line.

Almost immediately, a stretcher was being brought through, paramedics were on the scene. Juan didn't leave. Bettos didn't leave either, looking crazed.

Maya elbowed her way to the front of the crowd that had gathered.

There in front of her was a miniscule boy, being hoisted onto a stretcher. His lips were blue. The paramedics knew exactly what they were looking at. Maya knew this little face. She recognized the child, but from where? Her mind was flashing forward and back, trying to point to why this little boy was so familiar to her. She remained puzzled, but could not tear herself away.

Maya looked up to try to meet Juan's gaze-perhaps he could help. He'd always seemed like quite a civilized gentleman when Maya saw him in the school hallways or to discuss a Math Tutor for his son.

He was gone. Bettos was gone.

Maya realized.

Grief came over her like a wave of sea spray.

She looked back, the first time she had seen Death close up

* * * * * * * *

Chapter 21

Realidad

"I hate cameras. They are so much more

sure than I am about everything."

-John Steinbeck

Sofia turned on the news to clean. She heard a disturbing report about a death that had occurred in the Puerto Vallarta airport the day before. The young boy, only about 7 years of age it said, was still to be identified. His parents had not been located to be notified.

* * * * * * * *

Maya's thoughts were sharp as she was interviewed by USA Today in a small suburb, just outside L.A. the next day at her parent's home.

'You never felt so sick the day as you saw the 7-year-old boy, used as a drug mule, being taken away in an ambulance, already pronounced dead, his stomach full of balloons of Coke. They exploded once his young stomach acid eroded those sacs of Mind Candy. You never saw death so sick and in your face as you did the day you went on your vacation from teaching school kids in Mexico via Puerto Vallarta. You saw that tiny boy face before they pulled the cover up over it. The face itself as blue as the plastic cover used to conceal it.'

Maya felt knocked in the stomach, winded by the phenomena we all know as reality. Clarity descended upon her so rapidly she could not breathe enough air to keep her thoughts balanced. She shook her head as she saw she'd been foiled, used for the best parts and tossed aside a part of something she did not sign up for. The upended feeling of being fleeced by betrayal seeped into her temples.

She wondered if her hair was wild when they interviewed her. She hadn't slept.

* * * * * *

Post Script

Correro

'Among all forms of mistake,

prophecy is the most gratuitous.'

-George Eliot, from 'Middlemarch', circa 1871, (ch. 9)

     Drug production in Central and South America has a major impact globally. Supply and demand can be easily depicted by looking closely at consumers on any given Friday night: from small towns to larger places on the planet. In North America, we have the luxury of studying the effects of certain drugs on people south of us; it is a core part of the basis of the nation.

They produce; we support. Everyone suffers the consequences.

A nation's given mental and physical fitness and, ultimately, its bank ability, could even be correlated to a population's use of cocaine.

'It', being Narco Traficante or the route some narcotics travel to get to their ultimate resting place: the human nostril. Cocaine is the substance for which the most notable facts can be spilled. One line of coke affects the motility of male sperm for up to five years after it's used. Coke can cause addiction after the first time it's used. Cocaine affects the nervous system, beginning with facial ticks, and involuntary spasm, in ways that can be irreversible. Cocaine wears down the nervous and immune systems rapidly. A person with residual cocaine in their system 48 hours after its initial use may still be affected by the drug. Theses effects may include: nosebleeds, nausea, vomiting, digestive irregularity, erectile dysfunction, headaches, blurred vision, temporary loss of co-ordination/motor control and a host of psychological effects, include mood swings, irrational behavior and violence.

Any nation's medical system will be impacted with the use of cocaine where it is available. That speaks more to the inability of its users to use the drug with 'discipline'. It is too enjoyable to be enjoyed in small amounts. This, in the end, keeps doctors, social workers, nurses, lawyers, police, paramedics and other triage busy and working.

A Naturopath refers a patient who has come to see her for help to a dentist. That patient goes to the dentist to find what can only be described as a Rivulet Spanning Effect on dental issues from gum rot to tooth grinding. An infected mouth is a diseased person. The health concerns will only *begin* there.

Cocaine is considered by many the way to keep a party rocking. Thousands of young attractive, well-intentioned, smart young people use the white powder, more than excited for its arrival at a Friday night soiree. Coke has fans from all walks of life. Where it is available for sale worldwide, it remains top of the market, a sought after luxury enjoyed buy those with a six-figure income in North America. It keeps folks with lesser means in insurmountable debt for years.

Yet it's anything but rich. It's a low-life drug at its core, one that kills on its way to the consumer before it also kills the consumer. Steppenwolf wasn't kidding about the kids 'walking 'round with tombstones in their eyes.' Who can give it just one shot? It's a low-life drug ultimately, that murders on its way into the hands of the consumer. Before it continues in its ruthlessness...and also offs the consumer. The irony is, the story of the drug and how it got all the way to places like Canada or the US, would turn the stomachs of many of its buyers.

It begins its life as a leaf, growing abundantly off a plant. The plant is native to Central and South America, and can be found in other areas of the globe, also. The plant provides other such addictive substances as coffee and cocoa. As such, the cocoa plant is revered in Mexico.

The plant in nature alone is the basis of ups on both sides of the line; legal and illegal highs. Where would be without chocolate? Coffee is the very thing that saved Seattle and Vancouver from months of rainy blues. Come now, it's not all bad.

It can be found in its raw state flourishing in armed, secured, heavily gun-protected plantations. This provides work for numerous people, as the area must be patrolled for cops or thieves 24/7. It is a piece of land that offers well-paying work for growers, watering staff, fertilizer-makers, security guards and operation owners.

Down the line, upon insertion of processing and refining operations, it becomes an acidic white powder, enjoyed by those able to purchase and interested in imbibing. This provides work for police on both sides of the equation: those in North America trying to *prevent* its entry, and also those in countries of production, getting paid off to keep the flow moving. Lest we forget the inevitable cycle of cops in every nation who confiscate and use; this is really another arm in both the moving and the production.

The producers themselves, even if they do not ingest cocaine, will do so by the very conditions they work in. Likely, if a study of this sort were done in a production facility, nasal, chest and breast cancers may be traced to minute amounts of daily inhalation.

The people who buy it need to have money in order to do so. Coke's desirability creates a black market economy that supports the country, as well as keeping the buyer busy generating cash with which to buy. Coke needs to be packed, shipped, received, distributed, collected on, stored, moved, emergency-stashed. In every leg of production, people are busy working and people are busy making money.

Other above-the-table industries simply cannot compete with how much toil it offers humans.

Is black-market production really so bad? Black-market generated money is, after all, reinserted into the system once the seller makes any kind of store purchase, from cigarettes to diapers. The system likes purchases. Legitimate purchases can be taxed. Coke heads need the things that many people do and more so- perhaps in even higher volume (Kleenex, sugar, condoms, bath time bubbles, for example).

Are our governments in North America *really* all that against it? It can be easily justified as a victimless crime. It's a system helper really, as much as a system abuser.

Hell, if a senator is using behind closed doors, he or she doesn't want that option taken away. If we really cracked down the way we ought to save lives and large scale trouble, we'd lose a ton of system cash, cash we can't afford to lose.

Brings to light the very raw question of public safety if we cast that light on it.

All the while, people are busy being addicts and so the price will not be driven down; the supply will be needed as the demand remains fierce.

All the while, the addicts will need places to go to recover and so private recovery from addiction centers flourish.

All the while coke can be used as a creative tool, even as addiction besets the user. Some of the world's most amazing art can be attested to the false energy provided by coke.

Some of the world's best songs were written while the recording artist was high on coke. The entire production team may have completed a grueling, details-oriented recording session...while high on you guessed it.

Even tabloids benefit in print sales when celebrities cannot use with discretion or get in over their heads. So, it's worth its own weight in gold, if only economically.

Ethically, well, there's another story. The hosts of ill-effects psychologically are so big; we face a serious moral dilemma as a human race when people become 'infected' with cocaine. It alters behaviour and body symbiosis. If examined close up, we have the people that use coke and the people that don't. The two kinds of people do not function the same way. Coke, due to its expense alone causes rifts in humanity that are disgraceful. For example, would you like your child's teacher to be a cokehead, even if only s Saturday night user? Should you have to see a doctor who's wired? But you kind of *expect* the lead singer to be on it at the rock show. And the bouncer, well, he's gotta get through the night, right?

As She, the Snow Queen, moves through the veins of the world as both seducer and provider, we must acknowledge the many lives She touches.

Coke wreaks havoc on the health of consumers. This works to feed the System as a whole, too. The cumulative medical bills, shopping sprees, and alcohol-infused evenings hold a lot of possibilities for secondary generative money-making. Money that the System can really use.

The local late-night doughnut shop *wants* people to get sugar cravings from Coke abuse. So does the strip club.

Boosts sales.

* * * * * * *

Juan's life was about ensuring deliveries. That was Juan's part in the entire movement. A cartel does not exist in one place alone. Juan was just another critical player in a multi-faceted cartel. Juan *was* Narco Traficante.

Juan and Bettos were last seen taking a night driving voyage back to Guadalajara, where some more had been received. A week later, they reportedly had plans for to Sinaloa. It would be received again and distributed as it had been for some time.

* * * * * * *

Epilogue
Despues

A letter arrived with Damaris' family in Mexico, 6 months later.

'Wow, Damaris! Ms. Coleen just wrote me to say that you had recently won a big scholastic conference contest about your cumulative knowledge and understanding of academics. That is wonderful news! I am so happy for you, Damaris! Good work!

How are you? How is your nice family? I will always love your family. Such good people.

We decided together to come to Canada to work this year. I live in a very pretty place right now. It's right near a dock where my boyfriend and I go out in a our little boat to catch *cangrejo* (crab). We cook them up and eat them for dinner when the weather is not wild, west coast and stormy. I live close to nature, a nice little peaceful life. It is cold and quite wet/rainy a lot of the time, but when the sun comes out, my little city, is very pretty. About 1700 people live in my town. It's more like a *pueblo* really. VERY different than big GDL.

We decided to go to a different country for my next teaching assignment after Mexico. I had to apply to come here since I'm American. Zach loves to surf. We have to wear full wetsuits here in the green water to go out there in the surf. It's VERY cold. Colder than winter in Guadalajara. Our town hero, Pete DeVries won the last two surf competitions we've had here, the Cold Water Classics.

I have some big news! Zach and I are expecting our first baby this December! We are so excited! I feel great. I have a small belly, but not too big yet. Please tell your folks.

We are going to get married, too, but we're waiting until the baby had been breast fed for at least a year and is ok to eat solids. Then, I can have a little glass of tequila for the celebration. Also, we want to have REALLY good food there for our guests and LOTS of it, so we're saving $ to pay for it.

I love you always and send the best every day, even the tough ones. Remember, life is not always easy, but you have all the stuff you need to make a really GREAT life. Please stay in touch if you ever want to come work or live in my country...who knows what life holds?

xoxox, Maya, your American teacher'

* * * * * * * *

After the school year ended in Canada, they returned to L.A. together. Maya took a summer job at a local hotel/restaurant chain to make sure they had enough money to be parents for awhile. At the same time as she would be on a baby leave, Matt was starting his own IT business.

During her first month of work, it came to light that she was working for a hotel that was supported by a massive cocaine smuggling operation through Mexico.

THE END

Acknowledgments

Thanks to Mexico, in her struggle and her beauty; in her pain but with her vast and ancient wisdom. Massive gratitude to Clark, Tyler, Maggie and Charlie for helping me make it through the year. Charlie, thank you for making me laugh frequently. And for the photos. Big thanks to Andy and Stina Keiffer for making me comfortable and bringing their joy. Thanks to all the students I have known and loved, all over the world. Hug and thanks to Batman the cat for his constancy, and to dear Matty, of course.

Thank you to 'Cafes Moka' coffee houses of Mexico, who make the world's best Torrificada. Thank you *so* much to Teresa, Maren and Nava for being solid Goddess friends and to Shelley for her wisdom and humour. Thanks, to Julia: forever. Thanks to Gordon Thomas for grace and clarity, to Daryl Wakeham for his talent, to Dougal Fraser for all he has given to so many refined students of language and philanthropy. Thank you to all the thespians.

Thank you always and forever to Brian and Jack, whose sharp wits I adore. Thank you, Ben and Jacqueline for your enthusiasm and your adventurous spirits. Thank you, Val for clarifying those Mercury Retrogrades for me. Thank you, Kathy Poitras for your beautiful art images. Thank you, Laurie, for being my initial interpreter of the land and for your stories of incredible insight. Thank you Gordon and Morgan for showing me life with no fear. Thank you to Valerie Dunsterville for encouraging me to stay in school.

Thank you Lindsey for your spirit and the fun we had. Thank you Andy and Kathy Eisen for being the kind of people I would like to be. Thank you, Lara, for all the breaths of fresh air!

Thank you so deeply much to George and Harcourt for being there every step of the way and fleshing the book out with me. Really, big *big* thank you for your dear hearts, fine brains and love of those sweet animals. Thank you, Pam and Anne, my dear women, for your years of encouragement. Thank you Susan D for helping me in rough waters.

Thank you, Fraser. What a good man. Thank you Chelle, always.

Thank you very much to Margaret Howel for being my favourite English teacher and for inspiring me to keep at it. To Jason and Kaeli at Tacofino for all the great eats and words of encouragement. Thank you to Papa G for years of fun and intellectual splendour.

To my muses: kiss, hug and thank you to Suzanne Buffam for her splendour and loveliness, to Shiral Tobin, who does it all while being a gentle, clever diplomat. Thanks to Lisa and Artie for feeding me and employing me at SoBo, for your amazing family, and for helping me learn and grow. Thank you Glen, for shelter, for laughs and for your best.

Thank you for the good food, Organica, and all my lovely friends' tables of feasts to stay inspired.

* * * * * * * *

Thank you to Haley Marshall for her artistic grace. Thank you to Steve Dawson, his family, and to Jesse Zubot for the music. Thank you, Jay, for being excited with me.

Thanks to the extraordinary Leah Robinson for the lovely image, *'Truth and Beauty'* on page 5.

www.leah-robinson.com

Thanks you to the University of Victoria. Thank you to the Writer's Guild of Canada. Thank you to the Government of Canada. Thank you, Tofino.

And, to my family: thank you big from my heart to Jonty, Daniel and Anna, my siblings who guide and love me. Thank you to Aubrey and Heather, who bring the light and the real motivation for it all. Aubrey, especially for your ineffable drumming skills.

Thank you to the Green Goddess, Tara.

Thank you to Queen Saba, the cat. Thank you, Oakley. Woof!

And a very special thanks:

Thank you, Dada, for being one in a million-a fully inspired, capable human darling.

Thank you, Mama, for your belief in love of language and your encouragement to read and write from an early age.

Thank you, Johnny, for being my baby Daddy and for being pure Awesome.

NOTES:

Rachel Sutton, the daughter of European immigrants, was born in a small town in Alberta, Canada, and grew up in Vancouver, BC. She studied at the University Of Victoria, BC, and later became a multi-disciplinary student for many years.

Rachel initiated her studies majoring in English and Literature. She moved into Education and Child and Youth Care, where she later spent many years as a teacher and a social worker in more remote communities of BC, Canada.

She returned to school to study Herbology, Naturopathy and Ashtanga-Iyengar Yoga and then certified in those disciplines. She is known locally and through small pockets along the coast of Mexico as a healer, Yoga teacher and writer of science-based articles and recipes to promote human health. She is also known in some local circles as a social/political comic on air in broadcast journalism.

Rachel lives in a small cabin near the water in west coastal BC. She is expecting her first child with her husband, John Dawson, in December 2010. They live together with Oakley, the guard dog and Batman, the black cat.

This is Rachel's first novel.

Edwards Brothers,Inc!
Thorofare, NJ 08086
08 December, 2010
BA2010342